On the King's Sea Service

by

Richard Testrake

Cover photo Copyright:
<ahref='http://www.123rf.com/pro file_basel101658'>basel101658 / 123RF Stock Photo</a>

Copyright 2013

Richard Testrake

All rights reserved.

Dedicated to my wife Peggy, my daughter Lisa and my son Charles.

Table of Contents

CHAPTER ONE	6
CHAPTER TWO	21
CHAPTER THREE	36
CHAPTER FOUR	54
CHAPTER FIVE	62
CHAPTER SIX	74
CHAPTER SEVEN	81
CHAPTER EIGHT	98
CHAPTER NINE	109
CHAPTER TEN	115
CHAPTER ELEVEN	122
CHAPTER TWELVE	133
CHAPTER THIRTEEN	144
CHAPTER FOURTEEN	152
CHAPTER FIFTEEN	168
CHAPTER SIXTEEN	182
CHAPTER SEVENTEEN	203
CHAPTER EIGHTEEN	213
CHAPTER NINETEEN	222

CHAPTER ONE

Early Years

Summer 1782:

The ship-sloop HMS Athena, a French built 18 gun former corvette, now in British service, was beating against a brisk breeze out of the south east off the east coast of America, just off Virginia. She was on the starboard tack, thrashing right along when the lookout in the maintop reported a sail hull down on the larboard bow.

Captain Evans, his ship on a westerly course, immediately ordered it put onto the larboard tack. Evans was on his first cruise since he had attained the rank of commander and the position of captain of his own ship. The war seemed to be winding down now after the defeat of Cornwallis the year before and many ship owners were jumping the gun, trying to get their ships and cargos to sea early, in order to get the best prices for their merchandise.

The brig Emily Jane, was such a ship. She had been tied up in a Georgia creek for most of the war, the owners losing money every year and the brig deteriorating hand over fist.

With many ships of the Royal Navy being diverted to European waters and other parts of the world, the owners felt they now had a good opportunity to get a cargo to sea and hopefully delivered safely. They gave her hull and rigging a lick and a promise, filled her with tobacco and whiskey and she set sail for Philadelphia.

Captain Evans had been fortunate with his cruise so far. He had made three captures, giving each prize a crew and sending them to his base at English Harbor, in Antigua. Now he had a problem. He had already sent away most of his officers. There were few men left aboard HMS Athena who were capable of navigating, let alone bringing a strange ship safely into port.

The Emily Jane, heavily laden, low in the water and slow, had no chance against the rapacious ship-sloop. As soon as the Athena came booming alongside and fired a six pound shot across her bows, the slatternly brig let fly the sheets to her sails and wallowed to a stop, her crew running below to scuttle a whiskey keg to fortify themselves against their new ordeal, before the British prize crew came aboard.

Looking for a man he could spare to captain the prize, his eyes fell on Midshipman John Phillips. Phillips has served at sea for some half dozen years and had recently passed his board for lieutenant's rank, but had not been commissioned. Phillips was a capable enough petty officer, but in no way outstanding. Evans thought he would never be promoted to the glory of lieutenant's rank. He did his tasks correctly but had no important patron behind him to push him along.

As it happened, Captain Evans had a young nephew serving as his servant, who was available for a midshipman's appointment. The lad was his elder sister's son.

She was married to a family member of Mr. Townsend of the House of Commons. If he sent Phillips off commanding the prize, he might well never see him again.

This would give him an opportunity to rate his nephew as a midshipman in Phillips place. Rating the otherwise rather useless boy would please his sister and her husband and could well have important benefits in the future. To advance further in the Royal Navy, it would be necessary for him to first be posted to the rank of captain. A benevolent Member of Parliament might well be an influencing factor.

At present, with the rank of commander, he was only called captain by courtesy. As a post captain, he would be one in fact.

Making up his mind, he ordered the word passed for Mister Phillips to report to the quarterdeck.

Phillips was standing by the section of guns he commanded, looking at the brig that had just come to heel. Since the death of his father the year before, the quarterly remittances from home had dried up. Because midshipmen were paid so little, his finances were in a terrible turmoil. His uniform, much patched and repaired, was now also too small.

He suspected the reason he had not been promoted after he had passed his board, was that his superiors felt he would not be able to afford a gentlemanly appearance in the wardroom. When the distribution of the prize money from the captured ships occurred, he would have cash in his pockets again. At the call from the quarterdeck, he turned the six pounder guns in his charge over to one of the gun captains and ran aft.

"Phillips" Captain Evans decreed, "since you have passed your board, I am going to give you're an acting commission as lieutenant and send you to the prize to command her.

You can take a few men and a couple of Marines with you. The ship's crew you will secure; send the officers here. Make your way to Antigua and report to the commodore there, or the admiral, if he hasn't left yet. Get over to the brig now. I'll have your chest sent over with a few more men."

Phillips had been in the Royal Navy long enough to know the acting commission was a sop to the captain's conscious. If he were able to see the brig safely to port, the chances were some other captain, needing a seasoned midshipman, might very well snap him up out of whatever receiving ship he was aboard. The opportunity of returning to the Athena could be slim. It might be weeks before Athena made her way back to English Harbor.

The promotion to acting lieutenant was just a few words on paper that Captain Evans handed him. They actually meant nothing until an admiral or the Admiralty actually gave him a commission. Any Royal Navy captain that needed an experienced petty officer could well tell him to forget about that acting lieutenant's commission and to take a party of men to slush down the standing rigging of the foremast.

Until someone of necessary importance came along and noticed him, he would just go back to being a passed midshipman. Perhaps if he was lucky, he might be advanced to master's mate.

The jolly boat took Phillips over to the brig. He had taken the gun crews from his section with him, as well as a few Marines. The ship's launch came over soon after with more Marines and a few more seamen. Midshipman Horton, all of fifteen years old, was left also to help him with watch keeping.

The Marines helped get the captive crew below and under guard in the forecastle. Two of that number were professional merchant seamen of American persuasion, who had also served on shipping from various nations of Europe. Upon learning they would probably go to the prison hulks as prisoners of war, the seamen decided they would like to volunteer to crew the brig.

The new acting lieutenant omitted to tell these crewmen that having volunteered, they were now members of the Royal Navy and would remain so, until the Navy no longer needed them. Sooner or later, they would get 'Read In' properly and learn the bitter truth. The merchant captain of the brig and his officers were transported to HMS Athena. Some of them needed a little help, since most had been helping themselves liberally to the ship's cargo of whiskey.

With the ship under control, Phillips ordered the British ensign hoisted over the Rebel flag, dipped both and proceeded south. The Athena turned north to do a little more hunting, but Phillips had no idea how another prize would be manned. As they passed the Georgia colony, an American privateer came out to question them. Phillips had long since lowered both flags and declined to identify his brig's nationality.

When the privateer showed its teeth, Phillips showed his. He had four real six pounder guns aboard, a little powder and a few shot. But he also had ten gun ports cut in the ship's sides, five on each beam. He had two real guns on each side. The other ports being filled with 'quakers', wooden logs painted black and posing as real guns.

His 'weapons' looked real enough to pose a question to the enemy captain; when the irritable privateer fired one of its guns ahead of the brig, Phillips ordered one of the brig's guns fired right back at the privateer. The shot missed, but struck close enough to the enemy's quarter to splash water over the privateer's quarterdeck. With that, the rebel captain decided to look for easier prey elsewhere.

Phillips found he had little time for relaxation on the voyage. He had Mister Horton to assist him, but soon found that he was of little use on deck. The lad's navigational abilities were almost nil and his calculations could as easily find them in the middle of Africa or North America as their actual location. He found though, a bosun's mate he had aboard, had once served as mate on a merchant vessel and knew the rudiments of navigation.

For days, he napped on the quarterdeck in a collapsible canvas chair he had one of the hands construct. After a week on the prize though, he became comfortable leaving the quarterdeck to the midshipman and the bosun's mate together and went below to inspect his new kingdom. Most of the brig, of course, was crammed tightly with cargo, with barely enough space for a rat to wriggle through, but there were some tiny cabins he could search. He found one he thought had been the domicile of the supercargo, by the amount of paperwork scattered around the cabin.

Thinking to increase the purchase price of the prize by improving the appearance of the brig and thus to increase the amount of his own share, he began to straighten the litter in the cabin. The bunk, instead of being a ship's hammock, was actually a box built into the side of the ship. He found the mattress fitted into a framework on top and that framework lifted out. Underneath, he found some folded clothing and at the bottom, a small, iron framed oaken chest. In the chest were a hundred Spanish dollars and a few foreign gold coins.

The proper course to take, of course, would be to have Horton called to the cabin to witness the find, then write up a description and turn it over when he reached Antigua.

However, even at his young age, Phillips was well aware of the corruption that often ran rampant in shore installations. Should he turn that money in, he well knew it would invariably find itself in some clerk's pocket. He took the money and put it into the bottom of his own chest.

Upon reaching English Harbor, Phillips reported to Captain Edwards, of the frigate HMS Diana. Edwards told Phillips the major portion of the fleet, including all the larger ships had deployed to Halifax for the hurricane season. He further advised the first item on his agenda should be to report to the Governor and get his orders concerning his next actions.

Normally, he would be seen by the Admiral Sir Hyde Parker commanding the station, but with that official's absence, he should report to the Governor instead. He was told, most likely he would be sent to the receiving ship that was providing quarters for the various members of incoming prize crews.

With the uncertainty of his immediate future, Phillips decided he must make the best use of his own resources. He decided to use his new-found money to fund a new uniform for himself. He felt he was at a major crossroad of his life. With a scheduled meeting with the Governor of Antigua tomorrow, he didn't relish going to the interview wearing his tattered midshipman's gear.

Since, he was indeed a temporary, acting lieutenant, it might be wise to purchase the proper uniform for that office. The expense might be wasted should he never be confirmed in that rank, but sometimes one had to gamble. A master's mate he met on the frigate's deck informed him of a tailor on shore who specialized in naval and military officer's garb.

Finding it the next morning, he went in the shop and inspected their used offerings. He found a used lieutenant's coat that had been taken in trade. More searching uncovered breeches that could be made to fit his body. He was forced to buy new stockings. He thought 'Nothing ventured, nothing gained.'

A senior official, seeing him in the glory of a lieutenant's uniform, just might be tempted to make him the real thing. After being measured, he was told the clothing could be altered and in his possession in a few hours. Giving them a few dollars to get them working, he walked down the street a bit until he found a pawn shop. There he discovered a utilitarian sword. Nothing ornate, but in excellent condition, perfectly suited to a brand new lieutenant.

As a midshipman of course, he was required to be armed with a dirk, a short bladed weapon not very different from a meat carving knife.

As an acting lieutenant, a sword would be the proper weapon to wear, although when the hoped for commission did not appear, he would be forced to put it away and belt on the dirk again.

He donned the new uniform in the tailor's shop and with the sword, left to visit the governor. While his new attire certainly was not glorious, it did look professional and no one could say he did not look like an officer. He found the Governor enjoying a cigar and brandy after a good meal and in good spirits.

General Mathew, Governor of Antigua, told Phillips he had important dispatches that needed to be transmitted both to the Admiral in Halifax and to the Admiralty in London. "Could the Lieutenant handle delivering them?"

Nonplussed, not at all expecting such a task, Phillips answered that, while he himself would be happy to do so, he was unsure whether the Emily Jane was the right vehicle. He reminded the governor that she was slow and fat and multitudes of American and French privateers were swarming, looking for prizes. He was unsure whether he could deliver the dispatches safely.

General Mathew waved his misgivings away. "No young man. We won't be able to send your prize. She will need to go through prize court proceedings and the Admiral would never buy an old merchant brig into the service at this stage in the war. I do have a craft though. She is, I am told, a 'topsail cutter', very speedy, a King's ship, of course."

"Her commander, an elderly lieutenant name of Maddox, is here being treated for his ailments and I am told wants to retire here in the sun, rather than return home to face the cold winters. I have not an officer on the station who I would wish to give the command to. Sots, the lot of them! Are you a drunk, lad?"

"No sir!"

"If you want her, I will give you orders to take command and sail her to Halifax and London."

Now unsure of himself, Phillips offered, "Sir, I am not sure of my depth here. I had only an acting commission to bring the prize brig here. I don't know if I have the authority to take command of that vessel."

The governor grunted, then called for his clerk. "Timmons, draw up a commission for Lieutenant Phillips here. He is to take command of the cutter, HMS Vixen in place of Captain Maddox. He should take on the proper crew, equipment and provisions and sail her to London, with a stop at Halifax. If there are any questions as to the proper form, consult with Captain Edwards's clerk."

General Mathew looked at Phillips gravely. "Son, I do admire your honesty. I sincerely hope your professional ability matches it. Actually, you do have the authority if I give it to you. I need to send these papers out and you're the only one I have available, unless I send the frigate, and I need her here. I have observed the young officers aboard the General Washington in the harbor and found none that looked dependable. You at least look like a naval officer. As soon as you read yourself in aboard the Vixen, you will be a duly commissioned RN Lieutenant."

After spending some time nattering with the naval aide in the outer hall about family and acquaintances back home, the governor's clerk approached Phillips as he stood by the door. "Sir, I have here your commission. I copied the form from other documents we have on file here. The governor has already signed it and you are ready to go."

Walking down the street, with perspiration already starting to soak into the pristine paper, Phillips heard a familiar voice calling. Captain Edwards of the Diana was sitting at a road side table nursing an interesting drink, a large umbrella over his head and a Black servant standing behind fanning the insects away and moving the sweltering air around,

Edwards explained the ingredients to Phillips. "It contains rum, island sugar, a little ground cinnamon bark and the juice of lemons and shaddocks. It's really quite tasty." A word to the servant sent him running to get another glass.

"As it happens, I am waiting for an acquaintance. Why don't you sit for a few minutes and have a cooling drink? How did you make out at Government House?"

"Sir, I wonder if you could give me a course to steer. The governor gave me a commission and orders to take a cutter to sea. I told him I was an acting lieutenant and was unsure if I had the authority to take the cutter to sea. He told me that I would become a real officer as soon as I read myself in."

Edwards held out his hand and Phillips gave him the papers. "And so you shall be, young sir. As soon as you can get yourself over to the Vixen and read aloud your orders to the anchor watch, you will indeed be a commissioned lieutenant and her captain. After you look her over, come and see me on board the Diana. I know the Vixen. Her captain has been ailing and the vessel has been stranded here for weeks."

"Other officers have been drafting men from her since she arrived. I doubt if she has enough men aboard her to win her anchor. Get statements from your standing officers as to her wants and needs. I am sure you will need some men to get matters going on board."

"Sir, I do have the men who came here with me on the 'Emily Jane' prize brig. Some seamen and a few Marines."

"You do indeed, Lieutenant. Go have a look at your cutter. In the meantime, I'll send a messenger over to the prize to send you the seamen. The Marines we had best leave there. I'll send you a few of mine until you are ready to sail, just in case some of your people do not like the change in administration. If you need more men, you can send someone to the receiving ship to pick out more. I can give you a chit for them, if you give me a list of names."

As it happens, I have a few people aboard Diana I may be able to let you have. A master's mate for one. He wishes to go back home. His father recently died and left him a trading vessel he wants to sail. Decide what your needs are and we will see what we can do for you.

CHAPTER TWO

Vixen

After searching the harbor, Phillips spotted the topsail cutter referred to. It was tied up in a muddy tidal creek, alongside an old dock, the Vixen rather more ramshackle looking than the dock itself. A young Black seaman stood by the entry port, but there was no sign of any officer. As he approached, the seaman said, "He'p you suh?"

"Phillips said, "I'm Lieutenant Phillips and the Governor has offered me the command of this vessel. Are any officers aboard her today?"

"Jus' the Master, suh. Ah kin fetch him in a jiffy."

The man disappeared down the after hatch and a moment later, a rumpled looking middle aged man holding a blue coat spread over his shoulders came out of the hatch. He was a bit clumsy coming through, since his left arm was in a sling. He was also rather obviously, a bit under the weather from drink.

"Ben Jenkins, Sir. I am master of this craft. Sorry I was not on deck to greet you. I had no idea an officer was coming aboard."

Phillips explained his conversation with the Governor. "Will we have any problem getting to sea?"

"Sir, I don't know. The vessel herself is sound enough, but we have no stores aboard, or hardly any men, either. Ever since Captain Wilson left us, ships visiting the port have been drafting our people away from us. We still have most of the standing officers, aside from the gunner, but the working crew is mostly gone."

"What about yourself? How did you come by that arm?"

"Well, at the time, I was master's mate aboard the Whippet, a non-rated brig. We had run down a Yankee snow that was trying to get out of Wilmington and she hauled down her flag when we showed her our broadside. Our Cap'n, Mister Berry, had me go aboard to see whether she was worth sending in."

"Their cook had been asleep down below and was pretty pissed when he came up and found the ship had been taken. He grabbed a musket that was laying where somebody had dropped it and fired. The ball damn near took my arm off. Thankfully, our sawbones was drunk and the bosun patched me up. If the sawbones had got to me, he would have took off the arm. Anyhow, when we got into port, the master on this cutter worked out a trade with the admiral, before he left. I came here and he went on the Whippet."

Phillips replied, "Very well, understand I am not your captain at this moment, but I will be as soon as I read myself in. It would be better if we had more of a crew aboard before I do that. However, it might be a good idea if the standing officers would start listing all the needs and defects, so we may get a start in getting them corrected before the Vixen does go to sea."

Jenkins explained about the men aboard the receiving ship 'General Washington'. "Every time a prize enters the harbor and is placed in the hands of the prize court, the men and officers are taken off and placed aboard an old, captured sugar transport. Usually the ships they come from, return and get them, but sometimes they get drafted into other ships that need men. If you want, I can go to the transport tomorrow and pick out some hands. The only real seaman we have now is Caesar, the hand that met you at the entry port."

Phillips was mildly curious about Caesar. There were plenty of Blacks in the Royal Navy, but Caesar had an accent that was strange to him. Jenkins explained. "He came with me from the Whippet. I think it was off the coast of Virginia when Cap'n Berry decided he wanted some oysters for his supper."

"We went cruising close to shore and ran down an oyster boat. Mister Berry bought a bushel from the boat and Caesar, the boat's crewman carried them aboard. Turns out he was a slave, owned by the fisherman. Somebody asked him if he wanted to go back and he said no, so our captain read him in and he is now a free Royal Navy sailor. It was right after that I was shot and Caesar was put to tending to me. When I came here, Caesar came with me. That oysterman was right livid, when we took Caesar."

"Is it normal practice aboard this craft to have a seaman stand watch by himself, with no officer present?"

"No sir, not usually, but we have so few people aboard, that we do what we need to do."

Hearing the sounds of a group of men coming along the lane to the pier, Phillips said, "That sounds like some men that are to be taken aboard today. I'd like it if you went to the entry port and did the honors."

After the hands from the prize crew reported aboard, Phillips asked Mr. Jenkins to call all crew members present to the quarterdeck. When the few remaining standing officers as well as the Black seaman he had met previously approached and joined the new hands, Philips came through the hatch and motioned the two Marines from Diana to stand beside him.

Unfolding his orders from the governor, he cleared his throat and read them aloud to the men. He was now officially the captain, with the power of life or death over the men. Most of the men treated it as an everyday occurrence, just about what had been expected.

Most of them ignoring the talking, were observing their new home and the strangers around them. Some of the men from the prize brig seemed confused with Phillips wearing an officer's uniform instead of his midshipman's togs and acting like a captain.

One of the men, wanting to get at the bottom of these proceedings, began to push his way forward. A Marine grabbed him, spun him around and shoved him back into the group. The master said, "Take his name, Sir?"

"Not now, Mister Jenkins. Men, most of you know me. Tomorrow, we will probably take aboard other men, before we go to sea. You have all heard me read my orders. I am Lieutenant Phillips, formerly of the sloop Athena, now I am captain of the Vixen. For those interested, I was given an acting commission by the Captain of the Athena, which was confirmed by the governor here. We will become more organized as we get the rest of our people aboard. In the meantime, all of us will behave like the experienced seamen that we are."

Selecting a seaman who had served on one of his gun crew's back on the Athena, Phillips called him. "Anderson, come here."

The wondering man came forward and after a second's pause, knuckled his forehead in salute. "Anderson, I want you to go into my cabin and maybe the wardroom, see if you can find me a table and a pair of chairs there."

The man disappeared below after an "Aye, Sir" and the table and two chairs were soon placed on the quarterdeck.

"Mr. Jenkins, would there be pen, ink and paper aboard the cutter?"

"Sir, I have such in my cabin."

After a promise to replace the items, Phillips and Jenkins sat down at the table. They needed to assign each man to a watch, hopefully at tasks for which the man had already been trained. The first list was very limited since there were not enough men to fill every task. Another list had to be made, listing the station of each man aboard under differing circumstances.

When they finished that, as well as they were able, Phillips turned the crew over to Jenkins and the other standing officers. The cook came forward and protested there would not be enough food aboard to feed the evening meal and the purser assured him they were short of the spirits necessary for the men's ration. Calling the standing officers together again, he reminded them that he had earlier asked for a list of wants and needs from each department.

He now told them he was ordering them, at the risk of their rate, to produce such lists.

With lists from the purser and cook in hand, he decided to visit first the Diana, then the George

Washington receiving ship. A ride in a two wheeled cart cost thruppence, which he thought was highway robbery. Luckily, Captain Edwards was aboard the Diana and immediately wrote out a chit for the required men and provisions.

He then went to the provisioning wharf where he was told he would need to bring the cutter there, right then. If he wanted the provisions soon, he would need to supply hands to load them; since there were not enough men available in the yard. Phillips suspected the superintendent hired such men on a casual basis and with the RN supplying the labor gratis, would simply put the funds in his purse.

The captured Rebel ship, George Washington, was packed full of crewmen and junior officers. He talked with a twenty year old passed midshipman, as Phillips himself had been a few weeks before. He did not explain to the man that hours before, he had had only an acting commission himself. Midshipman Crawford had been on the ship for a month waiting for the frigate he belonged to.

When asked, Crawford assured him that he was not at all anxious to rejoin his frigate and would be happy to sail with the Vixen, furnished of course, with the proper orders from the Governor.

Phillips went around the ship with Crawford, interviewing men. Phillips wanted no unwilling people aboard the small cutter, so wrote down the names of those who expressed their willingness. On the way back to the Vixen, they stopped by Diana, where he gave the captain's clerk the names of the people selected.

It was late in the afternoon when they got back at the cutter and the hungry, ill-tempered men unmoored ship and the Vixen made her way to the provisioning wharf. The warehouse where the superintendent kept his office was now closed, but a watchman, impressed by Phillips' uniform and paperwork, let them in. Phillips hoped that the superintendent might have put out the necessary barrels of beef, pork, cheese, dried peas and other provisions out for them, but this had not happened.

In the absence of any crew around, Phillips asked the master to witness that he had placed the proper chits under the super's locked door, then ordered the men to start moving barrels.

They rolled the casks out to the dock, then used tackle to swing the material on board. While the men were working, Phillips realized the sun was setting. It would take hours for the cook to prepare a meal from the salted and dried rations. Standing on the quarterdeck, he spotted a man, a boy and a dog driving a small herd of cattle along the dockside road.

Looking around, he saw the young midshipman that had come to them from the Athena. He sent Midshipman Horton, along with a senior hand to approach the drover and see if he would sell one of his charges. When the pair came back, the boy said the man would indeed sell a bullock. The hand interjected. "His price was way too high, Yer Honor. He wanted seven Spanish dollars. I told him you would pay five."

Sending the pair out again, this time bearing the required Spanish dollars from his dwindling hoard, they returned driving a terrified bullock, one who definitely did not want to leave its comrades. A gang of hands soon had the animal dispatched, cut up into mess sized chunks and dropped into the cook's copper. It would still be a lengthy wait for the meat to cook, but the men would not need to wait until the salt had been soaked from the preserved beef in cask and the men were able to smell the cooking meat while they worked.

Phillips decided the men would have a double ration of rum after they finished their work. This at least would put them in a better frame of mind.

The Vixen still had no gunner, but he had discovered a gunner's mate on the General Washington, that he suspected would do well. A Marine messenger brought a note from Captain Edwards. Phillips was ordered to report to the Diana frigate and advise him concerning his activities and any further items the cutter might require; Edwards still acting in lieu of the commodore who was at sea.

The next week saw them hurriedly getting the cutter ready for departure, after receiving repeated queries from Diana and the shore. When Vixen was finally ready in all respects and had received her pouches from Government House, she set sail as ordered. Sailing up the Leeward Islands, the crew had to be constantly alert for enemy privateers.

Both French and Spanish corsairs abounded in these waters, more or less legally. At least Sailing Master Jenkins thought most of them carried letters of marque. Any vessel caught preying on shipping, whether merchant or naval that did not have such a document was liable to be considered a pirate and treated accordingly.

Vixen dodged two such suspicious vessels on her way out of the dangerous region. Finally slipping past Cuba out into the Atlantic, Phillips felt more at ease. Following the Gulf Stream up the East Coast, they saw remarkably few ships, except for one French privateer who chased them for most of a day.

Their cutter being faster and able to sail closer to the wind, they finally ran his topsails under the horizon and sailed farther out to sea. The cutter had begun taking on water up forward as she sailed north and upon reaching Halifax, as soon as all the pouches had been landed, Phillips made arrangements to have the Vixen surveyed for underwater damage.

As it developed, the cutter had lost some copper up forward, probably months ago and the hull had become wormed in that area. It was necessary to empty the cutter, send the people to quarters on land and lay her on her beam on a sand beach so they could get at the leak. New wood, caulking and copper repaired the problem and finally they were able to refloat the cutter, fill her again with people and stores and report her readiness to go back to sea, weeks after her arrival.

It was a bitter, cold day in the Halifax winter when she sailed again. She had missed the admiral when she arrived as the fleet had sailed south again after the hurricane season had finished. The dispatches meant for her to deliver to London, had already left on a different ship, but the Royal Navy was always able to generate new paperwork and now she had a new collection of pouches in the miniscule captain's quarters.

In the difficult winter crossing of the North Atlantic, encountering one howling storm after another, the Vixen slowly worked her way across. Realizing Jenkins was a much better navigator than himself, he let the master handle the task.

Days would go by without sight of the sun or stars and it was a most wearing job to attempt to predict where they were at any point in time. Finally, Jenkins was able to get a sun shot at local noon and assuming their chronometer wasn't too far off, there was a rather good guess at their possible location.

Entering the Channel, they were spotted by a brig, which Jenkins was sure was American. Phillips thought they could take on the brig, but he was wary of the instructions he had received regarding avoiding prize-chasing. However, the brig ended up chasing them for two days. Normally the cutter would have been the faster, but in the present gale conditions, the lightly built Vixen had to reef canvas to keep from losing her gear, while the sturdier enemy crept up to them.

Phillips was sure they would lose the enemy brig during the first night, but next morning, there she was, hull down, on her starboard beam. Phillips had been given strict orders to avoid initiating combat and was worried about violating those instructions. He had been warned verbally and in his written instructions he must do his best to avoid combat with enemy forces. He was strictly forbidden to pursue potential prizes. In this position however, if he did nothing, they were apt to be taken themselves.

The brig had ports for sixteen guns, six pounders, Jenkins judged. The cutter had only ten, with the two forward guns being only four pounders. From the speed the privateer took in sail, as the wind increased, Phillips judged the craft had a large crew, well trained at that.

When asked his opinion, Jenkins allowed they would probably be taken if they did nothing. As they scudded along, the lookout shouted a squall was about to overtake them. When fully enveloped by the blinding flurry, Jenkins put the cutter about and as she came out, met the privateer on her leeward side, almost gunnel to gunnel.

The enemy's gun ports were closed on that side and her guns boused right up, so none could break loose in the squall. Putting double crews on his guns, Phillips got four guns on his weather side ready to fire. As they came alongside, he gave the order to fire. The gun captains did not attempt to use the flintlock firing mechanism, but used the old tried and true slow match in the linstock.

One of the guns got a dollop of water in its touchhole and that one did not fire. The other three guns did, at almost the same instant. The enemy lee gunnel was almost under water, but a wave heaved the brig up for an instant. Two balls hit the same strake, at short pistol shot.

In calmer weather, this strake would have been above the water line and the damage not immediately dangerous. In this case though, that strake was plunged a fathom under water immediately after being struck and the vessel began to settle. Dozens of men manned the sides of the enemy and grapnels flew to bind the ships together.

Phillips called 'All Hands' to try to repel boarders, but before the enemy could get across, a wave swept over the deck of the privateer, over a combing and down into an open hatch. Instantly, the vessel began to settle, their would-be boarders waist deep in surging water. Axes were busy aboard the Vixen, cutting the lines on the grapnels.

By the time the lines had been severed, the gale had passed them. The wind had subsided, but the sea was still high. With not enough time and not enough men at the pumps, the brig went down with a rush, Vixen managed to make its way back to a cluster of men in the water. She ran one man down while approaching, but managed to get lines down to some of the others, who were pulled on board.

They finally entered the Thames and made their way up the river to London, where Vixen moored in the Pool and Phillips reported in to the admiralty. An official there took custody of his pouches and he was told he might as well go home for a month or more since after the strenuous crossing it would probably be necessary to survey the cutter again.

His pay was brought up to date and he found some of the old Athena prizes had made their way through prize court and the funds released. The crew was allowed 'head money' for the captured crew of the privateer, but of course, received nothing for the sunken brig. With his father dead and his mother long missing, he used some of his new funds to take rooms near the admiralty. A month later, he received news that the ship was being paid off and was going into ordinary. The war was over.

CHAPTER THREE

Interlude

With the release of his prize money, along with his lieutenant's half pay, Phillips was financially secure for a brief period, but he knew he soon would need to economize and gain an income of some type. He haunted the Admiralty, looking for some position on a ship, without any encouragement. In fact, he was told rather firmly, he should cease his visits, just come around once every half year to collect his half pay. He was assured if a vacant lieutenancy became available; he would be notified by post. As the most junior lieutenant in the now peacetime Navy, he knew well an active posting was not at all likely.

He had been in the habit of eating in a small inn near the river that catered to people rather low on the economic scale, where he could get a simple meal and a mug of ale for a few pence. One day, coming there in uniform after a visit to Admiralty, a drunk-jostled him and spilled a quantity of some greasy food on his blue coat.

At first the drunk wanted to fight him, until a glimpse of Phillips with his hand on his sword hilt with the blade half drawn, cooled him down. The landlady rushed to the officer, telling him she would clean the coat and to please not add blood to the food stains. The drunk, facing the threat of a sword in the hand of a man who obviously knew how to use it, quickly decided to leave the premises.

The landlady, Missus Harkins, put him in in an empty room with a large ale and some steak and kidney pie in front of him. After Phillips had calmed down a bit and emptied the quart, he realized the landlady was not bad looking. While she might be a little heavy for some tastes, he liked a woman with meat on her bones and she had the appearance that she might not be too hard to know. He knew she was a bit older than he. Obviously she would never see her twenties again, but still, she was easy to look at.

When she came back, the grease stains had been removed with a chalk ball and the whole coat sponged. It looked as good as new. She was impressed at having a King's officer at her establishment and wanted to know all about his service. He embellished a few sea stories to tell her, which impressed her even more. After he finished his drink, she offered to get him another.

She protested. "I'm no Ma'am, my name is Mary and I like to drink gin." she said.

After switching to gin, John gave the short story of his life, as did she. It happened that her husband Ben owned the 'King's Arms' in partnership with the husband's brother, Amos.

Ben was much older than Mary and could no longer perform his husbandly duties, a subject Phillips did not want to know that much about. The husband's wits were also said to have been deteriorating also and her life was lonely.

After playing a little 'slap and tickle' with Phillips, she asked, "Where are you staying now, John?"

He told her about the room he was renting from the widow close by the Admiralty. She said, "John, I could board you here for half of what you're paying there."

Knowing a bargain when he saw it the deal was made. They spent a few pleasant hours before she started putting herself back together. "I have to go to the kitchen and start the evening meal. If you like, you can get your things and move in here now."

A few days later, with no prospects for any work appearing on the horizon, John Phillips was in the tap room with a glass talking with some regulars. An elderly gent everyone called Bob, was talking about his business. It seemed he had a horse and cart and he bought fish from the boats as they came up the Thames early in the morning, then delivered that fish around the better areas of town; generally to cooks of the higher quality homes who needed a good product for the evening meal.

With his gimpy leg, he could no longer get around well, so he was going to leave his business and go live with relatives. He needed to sell his cart and horse. A little discussion divulged the information that he had a grandson who helped him with the route and this grandson could be hired very reasonably.

Phillips travelled the route with the man and his grandson and was sure he could make a go of the business. He thought the route could be profitably expanded and the prices raised a bit. The boy was knowledgeable about the route and a hard worker. The cart, though shabby and in need of paint seemed sound. The horse was different. The old gelding was thin and all his bones showed. Phillips felt though that more and better feed would make an improvement there. Shaking hands they sealed the deal, John handing over a significant fraction of the funds he owned.

Early next morning, he paid the inn's hostler to give the horse a good feed. From him, he found the inn had a good barn, with stabling for those gentlemen owning horses. The hostler agreed to handle the animal's feed and shelter for a modest sum. He asked Phillips not to give the animal any more feed. He said with the poor feed the horse had received previously, there was the danger of founder if fed too much rich feed too soon. The hostler assured Phillips he could improve the horse's condition if given a little time.

From his talks with Bob, he knew the proper price to pay for the fresh fish and he did so. One of the fishermen, knowing an amateur when he saw one, tried to talk him into paying near retail price. Phillips declined.

Traveling the route specified by Bob, they normally sold their entire product by noon. Soon he began buying more fish and was able to slowly lengthen his route. For a while, he thought about buying another cart and horse and sending his assistant out by himself on a new route.

Soon however, problems developed. He started having trouble with street thugs. Some men wanted to collect 'protection' money from him. He began to carry his sword, then, a big horse pistol that Mary loaned him. A few severely injured thugs soon got the idea that robbery was not a safe line of work to be in.

Then, it began to be difficult to keep the product fresh in the heat of the day as summer wore on. He soon found that many of his upper class customers did not stay in the city during the hotter months of the summer, instead removing to their rural homes. Finally, he found it necessary to suspend his fish peddling business during much of the summer, reviving the route in the cooler autumn weather.

For years, he followed this strategy. Money did become scarce sometimes, but he had his naval half pay which served as an emergency cushion. Mary kept his uniform in pristine condition and he used it only for calling at Admiralty. By now, Mary's husband had contracted Wasting Disease and was no longer seen around the inn. She informed John his mind as well as his body had gone and the local apothecary had no hope for him.

By now, they were a couple and no one commented on their co-habitation. Nearly ten years after starting his business, he came upon bad times. He had to replace the horse and the problems with the business mounted. Forced to borrow money to survive, he found himself unable to pay it back. There were threats to have him sent to prison for debt.

Mary rescued him from that fate, but shortly after, the brother-in-law came back on the scene. He had been away on business for some time, but one evening, she came to their shared room in a panic. A letter from the brother had come by post today. The brother had received word that she was up to no good with tenants of the inn and he was coming to investigate. Any problems discovered would be taken care of immediately.

The solution, as Mary saw it, was for John to incite a duel with the fellow and kill him. Phillips tried to disabuse her of the notion. First of all, while he was still considered an officer, supposedly skilled in arms, the brother in law was not. The disgust of the city would be directed at the officer who incited a duel with an unskilled, elderly civilian, Should he kill the man, he told her he would soon have an appointment at Newgate Prison to have his neck stretched.

In a panic she left and went to her own room. Phillips saw her no more for the next week. She no longer presided over the taproom and Phillips thought it better to leave the woman alone.

Late one afternoon, on a cold January day in 1793, he came home, unable to sell all his fish. Phillips had been hearing rumors for weeks about dire events taking place in France, but paid no attention. It was most unlikely that he, an itinerant fish peddler would be affected. He ended up giving the unsold fish away to avoid wasting it.

Wearily making his way back to the 'King's Arms', he saw a woman standing at the corner dressed in multiple layers of clothing. Phillips was walking by the horse's head, to spare the tired animal the burden of his weight, when she stepped out in front of him. Startled, he stopped, as she called, "John, please wait."

It was of course Mary, in her idea of disguise. "John, please do not come back to the inn. I think I have convinced my brother-in-law the reports he had about us, were just idle gossip. He acts like he likes me and I think he may become more interested when Ben dies. I can't let him find out about us.

"Well, what about my belongings back in the inn? I can't afford to lose my uniform and sword."

"I'll take the horse and cart with me. Early tomorrow, I'll load your belongings into the cart. When your helper comes, I'll tell him you are already at the river and he can take the horse and cart and drive it to you. I will really miss you, but you need to understand we can never meet again. By the way, this letter came in the post today."

Stunned, he shoved the letter into his trousers without looking at it. Without a word, he handed her the reins of the horse and she left, without looking back.

With no destination in mind, he wandered after her, staying well back in the evening shadows. At the inn, he watched as she unhitched the horse and led it into the stable.

He waited outside until after dark, then crept inside the barn. The hostler slept there he knew, but Phillips also knew he consumed a half pint of gin every night to help him sleep. He knew there was little danger of the man waking and catching him. Burrowing into a pile of hay, he tried to sleep.

With little sleep that night, John rose early the next morning before the hostler. As he passed the horse, it nickered, reminding him it was time to go to work. Phillips kept going out the door. He walked slowly down the path leading to the river. Once there, he stood watching a boat slowly drift downstream. It reminded him of his naval service and he wished he were at sea again. Finally, he heard the sound of the squeaky right wheel on his cart, one that he had been promising himself he would grease.

His bewildered helper was sitting on the box driving and a large bundle was in the bottom of the cart. The helper was curious about the different routine today. Phillips had to explain he was no longer living at the inn and would have to find a new place to live. With no better idea of how to spend the day, he thought about taking the time off.

While thinking over his options, he idle thrust his hand in his pocket and found the letter he had stuffed in there the evening before. Pulling it out revealed a black seal which he could not recall ever seeing before.

It proved to be an official missive from the Admiralty. It seemed he was being offered a position as Lieutenant on active service and was required to communicate acceptance or to state the reasons why he must decline. He frantically tore open the bundle in the cart and among clean work clothing, he found his old naval uniform folded beside the bicorn hat and sword. Among the other items in the bundle was a packet of cold beef sandwiches and a leather purse. The purse held twenty golden guineas.

Thinking about his options a minute, he threw his bundle back in the cart and with Billy riding in back, drove to a barber's he remembered. There, they waited for the shop to open. When the proprietor opened the door, he asked about a bath and shave.

The man assured he could make him look and smell like an earl and took him in hand. After his bath and shave, he dressed in his uniform and asked the barber to dispose of the old, smelly clothing. The cart then carried the two to the Admiralty building.

Without thinking, he landed the reins to the boy and said, "Billy, I am going to go away for a spell and can't take the horse and cart. They're all yours, if you want."

Billy wondered, "What should I do with them, Mister Phillips?"

Phillips fished into his pocket and handed Billy most of the money he had made selling fish the day before. "Buy some fish from a boat. Just buy the fish you are sure you can sell. See if you can get somebody to help you."

Inside, he gave his name and showed the porter his letter. He was led into a large waiting room filled to capacity with other officers and told to wait until he was called. Hours later, a shriveled old gentleman came to the door and called six names, 'Phillips' was one of that number."

The men were led into a smaller room, with chairs placed along the wall before a sturdy table. Told to wait, Phillips covertly eyed his fellows. All lieutenants apparently between the ages of twenty and forty. He particularly noticed one individual.

A supercilious individual in his early twenties, one who was massively built. Most of the bulk being fat, not muscle. His very face quivered when he paced about the room. When they exchanged names, that one admitted, with his nose firmly in the air, that he was James George Mortimer, Lieutenant the Earl of Brumley. The good earl then took no more part in general conversation.

Finally, the fellow who had led them into the room returned, led by a Vice Admiral. This was a vigorous looking man, in his mid-fifties and appeared to have a no nonsense look about him. Parking his rump on the table, he started out, "Gentlemen, I presume you have all heard about the events taking place across the channel in France. What you may not know yet is the fools there have decided upon war against Britain."

"Since we hear they are chopping heads off nobility with a vengeance, I doubt if their Navy is in much of a state to oppose us, since so many of their officers are of that estate. I expect bosun's mates may be commanding some of their first rate ships. However, the Admiralty feels it wise to get some eyes looking over their shoulders. We are taking vessels, both large and small, out of ordinary and into commission, as fast as they can be manned. The clerks are drafting your orders right now. I will look them over, sign them and you will be on your way to your duty.

The men remained silent until a clerk came back with an armful of sealed documents. Phillips was ordered to Triumphant '74 as second lieutenant for a three year commission. Employment! No longer would he need to go out on freezing days, selling fish from door to door.

As the officers milled about sharing their elation, Phillips noticed the Earl's face seemed pale and sweaty in the cold air of the meeting room. Phillips felt sorry for the man, obviously ill, he probably felt he must remain calm and assured. The others ignoring the man, Phillips said to him, "My ship is in Portsmouth. May I ask where you will be going?"

Initially, the man glared at him, seemingly at his effrontery, but then his face softened and he said, "I'll be going to Portsmouth too. I'll be commander in ship-sloop Exeter of 18 guns."

The man was now a commander, or would be as soon as he read himself in. Phillips felt he should show a little respect to the man. "Good show, Commander. I will post down. Would you like to accompany me?"

The Commander Brumley glared at him again and said, "No, I will travel down in my own carriage."

Another Lieutenant had heard some of the conversation and said ruefully, "Well, what would you expect of an earl with all those names?"

Phillips answered, "Like it or not, he's a commander now and outranks us. He'll probably make post before the end of the year. One of us could well find himself on a ship he commands."

Having a week before needing to report, Phillips got a room in a nearby hotel, then went looking for seagoing clothing. He bought a good boat cloak and a new, better quality uniform coat, a new hat and two pairs of shoes, with a set of silver buckles. Equipping himself also with new breeches and stockings, he felt he was ready for the wardroom of a third-rate. Everything went into a new sea chest.

Tempted to purchase a new sword, he demurred, thinking his present weapon was of good quality and would serve him well in combat. He felt he did not need to spend good money to show away in social events.

Two days after ordering his gear, he set out for Portsmouth on the mail coach. For much of the trip, the coach was full and he sat pressed against the body of a huge woman who had apparently not felt it necessary to damage her health by bathing.

At Portsmouth, he found a man with a barrow to trundle his gear to the water where he bargained for a boat to take him out to his ship. The two oarsmen threw his chest into the boat and with a muttered 'give way' by stroke oar, they were off. There was a moderate chop in the port and Phillips prayed he would not succumb. Few things were more amusing to the crew of a ship than that of a new officer 'feeding the fish' while reporting aboard.

However, all was well; on the challenge of the midshipman of the watch, one of the men shouted 'Aye, aye' and held up two fingers. Pulling his sword behind him, so it would not foul his legs, Phillips grabbed the man ropes as the boat surged up on a swell.

He pulled himself up by his arms, while searching for a batten with his foot. Finding himself, he climbed the side of the ship, the task becoming easier as the tumblehome leaned inward. When he reached the entry port, he saw a lieutenant waiting for him, raised his hat in salute and requested, "Permission to come aboard?"

Phillips was escorted to the wardroom, where he was introduced to the other ship's officers. It had now been ten years since he had been promoted to his present rank and that seniority gained him the position as second officer aboard Triumphant. Being second only to the Premier, or first lieutenant, kept him immune from the juvenile tomfoolery of the more junior officers. Told he had missed most of the hard work the others had experienced getting the ship out of ordinary, he felt fortunate.

Looking around the huge ship, he realized how much he had forgotten in the past decade. He had served aboard a third rate fifteen years ago, but most of that painfully acquired knowledge had disappeared long ago. When the captain's barge appeared, bringing their lord and master to the ship, Phillips was standing by the watch officer to meet the worthy.

The captain was affable and invited Phillips to dinner that afternoon, along with another officer and midshipman. He felt the bad luck he had experienced for the past decade had dissipated and he might now experience some of the better variety.

Waiting in the wardroom for the appointed hour, Phillips heard the call, "Passing the word for Lieutenant Phillips. Second officer to the quarterdeck." Phillips put down his glass and raced up the ladder. On the quarterdeck, he saw the captain standing at the weather rail, talking to the officer of the watch.

He walked rapidly over and doffed his hat. The captain looked at him quizzically and stated. "We just had a strange signal from the flag. It told us to send a boat with the second officer. It also said for you to bring your gear. Sounds almost like you may not be coming back. Have you been doing something you shouldn't?"

The trip over to the flagship was puzzling for Phillips. Try as he could, he was unable to figure out anything he might have done that would have alerted the admiral. Perhaps his lack of experience had been realized and he was being sent ashore. He climbed the side of the huge first rate and reported to the ship's officer of the deck. He was hustled aft to Admiral Parker's sea cabin and told to wait. An elderly man came out and looked him over. "Phillips, eh?"

"Yes Sir"

"Ever command anything before, Lieutenant?"

"Yes Sir, Governor Mathew at Antigua gave me command of the cutter Vixen in '82. He ordered me to take her to Halifax and London to deliver dispatches. I also commanded a prize brig as an acting lieutenant."

"You ever met Commander Lord Brumley?"

"Yes Sir, I met him recently in London."

"Here is the drill, Lieutenant. Brumley has come down with some ailment. Sawbones says it has to do with his heart. Anyway, he is sick and won't be going to sea any time soon. Problem is, he commands HMS Exeter, an 18 gun ship sloop. His lieutenant was a midshipman last month and is not ready for command.

I want Exeter off the French coast immediately. I need someone who has successfully commanded ships before. Looking over your records, I did see you commanded an armed cutter ten years ago. But, I noticed that you have been on the beach since then. Do you think you could handle this command?

"Yes sir, assuming she is seaworthy and has a crew, I am sure I can."

"Very well young man, you are the new commander. You have a competent Master on board. He would be on a first rate by now, if he weren't such good friends with a bottle. If you can keep him sober, there is no better man alive at navigating and handling a ship. Remember, you can trust him sober, I have myself."

"Yes Sir."

"Just a little warning. You are being promoted due to your previous experience long ago with command in wartime. Should you not succeed in this command, there are precious few openings for failed Royal Navy commanders. As a lieutenant; yes. In time of war, it would not be difficult for you to secure a position."

"Now, you have been brought forward because of naval necessity. Some of the other lieutenants on this station have years more sea time than you do. Each will feel he himself should have been selected instead of a relatively inexperienced officer like yourself. I picked you because you do have command experience in war time conditions. Remember, you are a commander now, superior in rank to your former comrades. Now, did you bring your sea chest?"

"Yes Sir. It's still in Triumphant's boat, alongside."

"Very well." The Admiral turned to a servant and ordered, "See the captain. Tell him I would like our new commander's sea chest transported to Exeter without delay. Commander, beg a boat from the officer of the deck. I'll give you permission to go ashore to buy a swab. In an hour, I expect to see a signal flying from Exeter asking permission to sail if the wind is suitable; the pilot will be waiting for you when you come back from shore.

Admiral Parker added. "Your orders are being drafted at the moment. My flag lieutenant will have them sent to Exeter, while you are ashore purchasing your swab. Read them carefully and follow your instructions. In case any difficulty arises you find you have no instructions for, remember you are now a commander in the Royal Navy and are expected to make correct decisions at a moment's notice.

CHAPTER FOUR

HMS Exeter

The flagship's jolly boat dropped him off at quay side near the naval outfitters. He rushed inside and told the proprietor he needed to purchase an epaulette right away. The man showed him a selection of varying quality. Unsure of what his immediate expenses would be before he could get an advance on his pay, he selected the cheapest one available, knowing the salt air would probably turn the ornament green in weeks, if not days.

The proprietor asked, "What ship, Commander?"

"HMS Exeter, anchored near the flag."

"Oh yes. I thought Lord Brumley commanded her?"

"Well, he did, but a medical emergency put him ashore and now I have the command."

"Commander, I realize newly appointed captains sometimes have difficulty purchasing the necessary items needed for the start of a new commission. We would be glad to extend credit for any necessary purchases you might wish to make." Phillips told the man about his time restraints. "The admiral expects me to be prepared to put to sea in a few minutes. I don't really have much time." "Sir, have you a boat?"

Looking out the window, he saw the jolly boat was already halfway back to the flag.

"No, I do not. I'll need to engage a shore boat to get out to my command."

The proprietor called an assistant over and whispered in his ear. The man ran out of the door as fast as he could go. "Sir, we have a boat to transport you out to the Exeter."

The man then pointed to a display of goods piled in a corner. Cases of wine and spirits, cheeses and crates of biscuit, casks of preserved foods and the like.

"Captain, we have here a selection of goods many new commanders find necessary at the start of a commission. Should you decide to purchase these items on your credit, I would be pleased to allow you this better quality epaulette gratis."

When Phillips nodded, there was a flurry as a crowd of workers hustled the goods out the door into the boat which had magically appeared. The proprietor himself fastened the shiny new swab on his left shoulder. Phillips settled himself in the stern sheets of the boat, beside the coxswain. The cox'n nodded to stroke oar and growled, "Give way."

As they neared Triumphant, intending to pass, Phillips asked the cox'n to pass close by the ship. As they neared it, the challenge came over the water. The cox'n stood and shouted, "Passing." After the cox'n sat down again, Phillips stood shakily in the boat, opened his cloak, lifted his hat to the master's mate of the watch and shouted, "Jackson, would you please inform the captain that I've been given command of Exeter?"

A moment later, the Triumphant's captain stuck his head out a stern window and shouted, "You have a command? Come aboard and we'll open a bottle."

"Sorry, captain, I expect orders to sail at any moment. The admiral was most insistent there be no delay." Doffing his hat again to the Triumphant, he sat until they came alongside the Exeter. Again, they were challenged, this time the cox'n yelled, "Exeter", signifying the captain of that ship was coming aboard. By rights, of course, Phillips was not actually the captain yet and would not be until he had 'read himself in', but everyone felt he was close enough.

He was met by a lieutenant and the Marine detachment, those worthies emitting puffs of pipe clay from their whitened belts and straps at every sharp movement. A band of the ship's standing and warrant officers stood in a group behind the first officer. What looked like most or all of the ship's hands stood amidships. The lieutenant, shaven until his face was raw, introduced himself, "Sir, James Braddock, first officer, if you please."

"Lieutenant, would you please introduce the officers."

As they went down the line, Braddock spoke each warrant officer's name and the officer lifted his hat. When finished, Phillips asked, "Lieutenant Braddock, would you have the hands gather near the quarterdeck?"

When the hands were gathered, he handed the lieutenant his orders and asked him to read them to the crew. When finished, he addressed the crew briefly, "Men, I am sorry for the loss of your captain due to illness. I am sure he has trained you well and we will use that training to inflict upon the enemy such injury that he will not wish to come near England again."

In an aside, Phillips told Braddock, "Release the men, but keep both watches on deck for now. I expect sailing orders at any moment. Are we ready to go to sea?"

"Yes sir, we have our stores and are only lacking about ten men. However, many of the crew are landsmen and the seamen have not been worked up."

"Lieutenant Braddock, I seem to have missed meeting our master. Is he aboard?"

"Yes Sir, he reported sick and is in his cabin."

"Mister Braddock, once we get to sea, please see what you can do to get our people in a proper state. In the meantime, getting out of the harbor without embarrassment is the first of our priorities. Now, who is our signal midshipman?"

Braddock introduced a gangly midshipman, apparently a few years younger than the first officer.
He answered to the name of Mr. Midshipman Withers. "Mister Withers", Phillips ordered, "Signal the flag, HMS Exeter is ready to proceed."

There was a delay, while the nervous first officer went around the ship, pointing out defects to the appropriate people. Finally, the lookout reported, "Boat coming to us from the Flag."

Phillips removed a glass from the binnacle. The launch was indeed coming directly toward the Exeter. A figure in the stern had his cloak pulled down so he could see the gold epaulettes on each shoulder.

Warning the first officer they were about to be visited by a full captain, the ship was instantly in a state of turmoil, with everyone rushing to stow whatever odds and ends were adrift. As the boat neared, she answered the challenge by a shouted 'Majestic'.

Phillips raised his hat to the officer, wondering how he was supposed to entertain the man. His new stores had just been lifted on board and had still not been struck below. He had no servant appointed and he not set foot in his cabins yet. He did not even know if he had a table for entertaining or dining.

Deciding to take the bull by the horns, upon greeting the officer at the entry port, Phillips said, "Captain, I have just stepped aboard myself a few minutes ago and have yet to enter my cabin. I must apologize for my lack of preparation."

As Braddock came close and mouthed "Captain Raleigh" in his ear, Raleigh waved off his apologies. "The admiral and I both know how busy a captain is when he takes his ship to sea, especially for the first time. I have brought with me a basket of cold food and the admiral contributed a dozen of Madeira of which he is right proud. My servant can serve us, perhaps here on the quarterdeck, if you are able to supply us with a table and chairs. Thus we can watch, while your first officer takes your ship to sea."

Phillips beckoned his frantic lieutenant over and murmured quietly. "The captain wants to eat an early lunch here on our quarterdeck. Do you suppose we can have a small table with two chairs brought up? The Captain's servant will serve us."

The wretched officer nodded his understanding. Phillips elaborated, "The captain wants to see you take the ship to sea, while we dine. I realize this is a horrible spot to put you in, but I am as helpless as you are. If you wish, you can tell the men they will get a double ration of grog, once we are at sea, if we can pull this off without crippling ourselves."

In a matter of minutes, the wardroom servant and his mate had delivered a table and chairs to the quarterdeck and the fascinated crew observed the visiting servant setting the table with a snowy cloth and gleaming silver.

The food was merely a pair of cold roasted chickens and cold roast beef. A loaf of crusty bread, fresh from the shore side ovens was sliced by the servant and the two set to, watching the ship win her cable, while Madeira wine was sipped. The men on the capstan bars using every bit of effort their bodies could generate slowly pulled the ship up to the anchor. "Up and down." shouted a master's mate stationed near the hawse. Then he shouted, "Anchor a trip."

With the ship still moving ahead from the impetus of the capstan, Braddock announced, "Hands make sail." Topmen scrambling in the rigging loosed the big sails to catch the forenoon breeze. The capstan pawl clicking more rapidly now, the anchor rose toward the hawse. While seamen secured the anchor to the cathead, landsmen on the braces trimmed the sails to the breeze. Gradually, the slowing ship, began moving ahead under the force of the wind.

Captain Raleigh wiped his lips with a napkin. Putting it down, he addressed Phillips and Braddock, who had come over to see about new orders. "Gentlemen, I am very pleased with what I have seen today. You have an excellent ship and a capable crew. Please accept the remains of the food and wine with my compliments. I have not seen your sailing master in the activities today. The same old problem, I suppose?"

"Sir, the master has reported sick this morning. I have not had the opportunity to ask the surgeon about his status, yet,"

"I see. Well, good luck gentlemen."

Braddock ordered the main topsail backed, in order to take some of the way off the ship, while Captain Raleigh stepped down into his launch. Phillips saw his people had entertained the visiting oarsmen very well. More than one caught a crab with his oar as the boat crew tried to cope with the chop.

CHAPTER FIVE

Locating the Enemy

At sea, Phillips ordered: "Mister Braddock, please set course for Le Havre. We will report to the Channel Fleet off the coast there. After we are squared away, have the purser issue the grog, a double issue today I think, then send the hands to dinner. If you find someone who you think might do as my servant, please send him to me after dinner. Now, I believe I will go to my cabin, to see what I have to work with."

A Marine was standing tall outside his cabin, as stiff as a statue. He addressed the man. "What is your name, Private?" The astonished Marine, trained to keep his mouth shut, considered, before answering, "Burns, Sir."

"Very well Private Burns, There will be times when I need to call for someone. If I do, you are to repeat my call."

"Aye aye Sir."

"And, any time your sergeant or one of my officers is not around, feel free to scratch your arse if you need to."

The dumbfounded Marine could not utter his standard "Aye aye Sir." He made a sort of nod and remained at attention.

In his cabin, Phillips found his gear including the purchased cabin stores from the naval outfitters piled in the center. Other than that, the place was empty. In the sleeping cabin, there swung a hanging bed, basically a shallow wooden box hanging from the overhead from a line to each corner.

While he was trying to make some order from this state of affairs, the Marine at the door shouted, "Landsman Jones, Sah."

A wizened little man of indeterminate age entered his hat in his hands. "Silas Jones, Sir", he muttered.

"Well. Jones. What can I do for you?"

"First officer sent me sir." "You

are to be my servant, then?"

"Dunno Sir, Maybe, Sir.

"Well, we'll give it a try." Going to the door, he asked the Marine to pass the word for the carpenter. When the carpenter stood in the door, knuckling his forehead, he asked him what could be done to store his belongings out of sight. Chips said, "Captain, the Lord Brumley had a pantry next to the bread locker that he kept his food and wine in."

"That's still there. Now, when we took the ship out of ordinary, there were little lockers fitted in all around your cabins for clothes and belongings. He had me tear them all out and he had shore side

cabinet makers make some fine mahogany cabinets.
I could have told him they wouldn't stay in place in any sea way, but he generally wouldn't listen. When he got sick and went ashore, his people came on board and took all that out."

"Have you any recommendations?"

"Well Sir, I could rebuild her like she was before. Build all those cabinets and such?"

"That would be a good plan, Chips. Better get started."

Now was a good time to deal with the master. He seemed to be in very sad shape, when Braddock brought the man before him. He appeared to have worn the same clothes for days and at some time had vomited upon himself.

Braddock introduced him to Mister Avery, the sailing master. Staring at the man, Phillips observed, "Both Admiral Parker and Captain Raleigh told me separately that you were a great friend of the bottle. We will be operating off a hostile shore, often by ourselves. The ship greatly needs the services of a competent sailing master. Now, am I going to be able to rely upon you, or are you going to report 'sick' again just when I need you the most?"

"Sir, you can count on me. Mostly, I don't drink at sea. But sometimes on the shore, the need just overpowers me."

"Avery, I can't do anything about you now. We're on our way to report to the Channel Fleet off Le Havre. If you behave in any unprofessional manner though, I will have you standing in front of the admiral before you can spit. Are we understood?"

"Yes Sir."

"I dislike telling a man when he can or cannot drink, but it would truly be wise for you to keep the cork in the bottle while we are at sea. Dismissed, Sailing Master Avery."

Going out to the quarterdeck, Phillips saw they were by themselves in a sunny sky, under a topsail breeze. Braddock had the deck and Phillips waved him over. "You've been on deck since we left Portsmouth. Who's to relieve you?"

"Well, Sir, generally the Master and I have alternating watches, but with him being sick..."

"Sick, my arse. The man was drunk. Send somebody below and get him up here, then go rest, yourself. I'll be in my quarters."

Avery reported on deck and relieved the lieutenant. Phillips saw he had attempted to shave, but had apparently been interrupted while doing so. Patches of beard and drying smudges of soap mottled his face. By standing on a chair in his cabin, Phillips could look through the skylight in his quarters.

Observing, he saw one of the junior midshipmen making some antic gestures behind

Avery's back. A passing master's mate stopped and apparently chastised the boy. After a moment, Phillips removed his coat and hat and went out on deck. Going to the helm, he checked the course and asked the helmsmen, "What was the problem a minute ago between the midshipman and the master's mate?"

The men were clearly hesitant to respond and one of them said, "Dunno, Sir."

Pondering a moment he went back to his quarters, speaking to the Marine at his door. "Private Burns, I don't know all the men's names yet. That master's mate on deck now, up forward, do you know his name?"

"That's Mister Ackroyd, Sir."

"Would you pass the word for him to report to my quarters, please?"

The captain heard several calls for 'Mister Ackroyd, report to Captain's quarters'."

A minute later, the Marine reported, "Mister Ackroyd, Sir."

When he said "Enter", the alarmed young man came in the cabin.

"Mister Ackroyd, I wonder what that exchange between you and that boy up forward a few minutes ago, was all about?"

"Captain, he thought Mister Avery looked comical when he came on deck."

"What would you recommend we do about it, Mr. Ackroyd?"

"Sir, if he were one of the other mids, I'd say we should masthead him."

"What's different between him and the other mids?"

"Sir, Captain Lord Brumley brought Mullins aboard with him. He is the son of a friend who serves in the Lords with him. We were told none of us were to administer any punishment to the boy."

"Mr. Ackroyd, since I am now captain, I will be making the decisions about administering punishment. For now, have Mister Mullins sent to whatever masthead you select. Make sure he understands about the change of administration.

His next infraction will cause him to kiss the gunner's daughter." Boys committing infractions, were often bent over a gun, the 'gunner's daughter' and beaten on the buttocks. As it was, young Mullins could expect to be exiled to the summit of one of the masts until either the captain or first lieutenant called him down.

The next few days were spent in training the crew. Hours were spent exercising the various specialties aboard, especially the gun crews. The coast of France was just in sight from the deck, when another mastheaded mid spotted a sail hull down right up against the land ahead.

As the Exeter swept in to investigate, her lookouts spotted the brig, pinned by the wind against the land in a little bay. She seemed at first to be attempting to beat out, but after spotting Exeter, she changed her mind and anchored.

A village stood against the head of the bay. Fishing boats dotted the bay, with one in sight just around a point, to their starboard. The Exeter stood away from the land and slowly drifted back out to sea in the light airs, keeping the separate boat behind the point just in sight as long as the light lasted.

As the sun dropped, the Exeter came back toward the last known location of the boat they were stalking. It had been drifting and was no longer where they had last seen it, but someone in the boat uncovered a lantern and revealed its position. Phillips had ordered the binnacle light covered and all other lights in the ship had been extinguished. The sloop ghosted right near the fishing boat before its crew heard the water burbling under the prow.

The first lieutenant had gone about the sloop before, to see if anyone aboard was fluent in the French language. Surprisingly, the only such person was the young Mullins. He had had schooling in Paris before the war and was fluent.

Phillips had him ask the boat's crew whether they would sell some fish. After animated conversation, Midshipman Mullins reported that, while fishing was poor tonight, they did have a few they would sell; the boat crew hurriedly threw some fish in a wood box and passed it up.

The only French coin available on the ship, were a few old silver livres belonging to crew members. Phillips traded a pound note for each coin. The French crewmen were excited about their good fortune, so Phillips asked if they would like to come aboard to have a glass of rum, or perhaps some wine. They gladly clambered up on deck and Phillips led the procession of French boat crew and Midshipman Mullins to his dining cabin.

Phillips saw that Chips had made great strides in getting his quarters livable. A long dining table stood constructed and Jones had spread a length of sailcloth over it. A problem arose, when it became apparent there was only one chair available.

The Marine was called into the room and helped Jones construct a makeshift bench from a board laid over a couple kegs of his provisions that had not been stowed yet. The Frenchmen were impressed with the strength of the rum and several toasts were drunk to the glory of France and long life to the Republic.

Phillips was uncomfortable with that toast, imagining the consequences that might ensue should his superiors hear of it. He comforted himself with the thought that since he knew no French, he had no official way of knowing what the toast amounted to.

Finally, Phillips thought the fishermen might be in the mood to answer some questions he had about the harbor and its defenses. Immediately, the camaraderie ceased. The individual Phillips judged to be the owner of the boat gave a harangue in impassioned French.

Mullins reported the French were insulted to be asked to spy on their village. It was obvious that the interview was over. As the group rose to go on deck, Phillips noticed that one of the group, younger than the others, was hanging back a bit. Phillips had the idea the lad did not want to return to the fishing boat.

In a quick aside to his translator, the captain asked him to see if the boy would like to go inspect the midshipmen's berth. The bewildered Mullins did so and the boy nodded agreement. The other two boat crew were now fuddled with the rum they had consumed and seemed not to notice they had lost one of their party. It was only after the two got into the fishing boat, that one started calling for André.

Once the boat was cast off and left behind, Phillips ordered Mullins and André brought back to his quarters. His questions were answered. It seemed the lad's grandfather, the old town mayor, had been visited by the local Committee of Public Safety. This was a group of loud individuals who had heard of that organization in Paris and thought it would be well if they could start a branch organization in the village. The idea being, they could use their imagined powers to rid the village of those who thought differently than themselves.

They showed the local blacksmith a woodcut of a guillotine as used in Paris and one was soon constructed. The machine had already been tested. It worked as expected. The first test victim was a trussed pig, the mayor was the second. André was adamant that he wanted to be away from France. He felt he also would be soon under the blade if he remained in the village. Phillips offered the lad passage to England, or any other destination in Europe his ship might go.

The boy said the brig they had seen enter the harbor was anchored under the four guns of a newly constructed battery. He did not know the caliber of the guns, but held up his hands, indicating the size of the ball. Phillips guessed the guns to be twelve or perhaps eighteen pounders.

Nothing like he would wish his little ship to face. For his ship to close the brig, or the town itself, they would first have to pass the battery situated on the side of the bay. Calling in the sailing master, they examined a chart of the area. The bay was located a little to the northwest of Le Havre. A stream running to the sea entered the little bay near the location where the brig was located.

Exeter was behind a thin peninsula that formed the southern limit of the bay. The chart showed a coast road that ran northerly past the rear of the village.

Releasing the men to their duties, Phillips ordered the French lad installed into the midshipmen's berth and the ship sailed out to sea. At daybreak, the first officer was called to the captain's quarters, along with the sailing master, now perfectly sober and capable, the Sergeant of Marines and the bosun.

A plan was developed. The ship would demonstrate in the bay its presence, perhaps firing a shot or two toward the shore. Obviously the crew of the fishing boat would have reported their presence by now, so there would be no loss of the surprise factor. At dusk, the ship would sail directly out to sea, far enough out that no one from shore, at however high an elevation, could possibly see them.

After dark, the ship would proceed to the far side of the peninsula and remain there overnight. Under cover of darkness, a landing party would be loaded into boats and sent to shore, hidden from the village by the intervening peninsula. During the night, they would proceed along the coast road until coming to the village.

If undiscovered, they would remain hidden until first light, when they would attack the battery from behind. If detected during the night, the attack would commence immediately if a successful attack was deemed practical. If not, the landing party was to return to the boats and come back to the ship. In the event of an attack, if the opportunity existed, a red rocket would be fired at the beginning of the attack, with a blue light to follow when the attack was deemed to be successful.

Boat crews would be left with the boats that had carried the men ashore. When they saw the blue light, they would proceed back to the ship, under sail if practical. It was judged best to leave the boats at the landing area temporarily in case something went badly awry and it was necessary for the attack party to return to the ship. If all went well, after picking up the nearly empty boats, the ship would proceed into the harbor and deal with any organized resistance.

CHAPTER SIX

First Blood

The next day was spent out of the sight of land practicing for the evening's work. The boats were lowered into the water to ensure the seams would swell and eliminate possible leakage. Men practiced lowering themselves into the boats, time and time again. When it was felt the ship and crew were as ready as they could be, the ship sailed for the harbor and up the bay 'till a shot from the shore battery warned them to proceed no farther.

Phillips decided not to return fire, since it seemed the enemy gun was an eighteen pounder and he did not want to advertise his relatively tiny six pounder weapons. He did however ask his officers to mark the location of the battery in comparison to the coast road, which they could see from the ship. Finally, he dipped his flag in salute and went back out to sea. That night found them at anchor off the other side of the peninsula, out of sight of the village and battery. The men's weapons were checked before they were loaded into the boats.

A buoy had been made up for their anchor cable. When the time came, rather than attempt to weigh with the few men left on the ship, they would slip the cable, its position marked by the buoy. The boats carried two dark lanterns. The light from the flame inside was hidden by tight fitting shutters. A lit dark lantern would be useful for lighting slow match for the firing of the pyrotechnics. In a pinch, of course, a little powder in the pan of an otherwise unloaded pistol or musket could also accomplish the same task.

A quiet "Goodbye" sent the boats off. After waiting for any last minute problems to arise, the ship slipped her anchor cable and proceeded to the area they were to wait. Few men were left on the ship. Phillips had agonized over whether he should remain on the ship, or go with the attack party. In the end, he decided he would best remain on board while Braddock and Ackroyd would go with the attack party. The night was unusually dark, there being a low lying overcast. The light breeze was from onshore, though Phillips judged he could beat into the harbor if it did not veer. Avery said he would stake his reputation on it holding steady. Withers, he kept on board, so he had another officer other than Avery to rely on.

Finally, just as the faintest hint of a sunrise came in the east, the crew could hear the sound of a distant bell clanging away, then the popping of muskets. Judging the fight had started early, Phillips gave the order to proceed on course to the pickup point. As the ship gained speed, they saw the red glare of a rocket and the shooting seemed to die down, although the bell kept clanging. Then, the blue light was seen. There was another interminable wait until the ship's boats appeared.

Phillips now wished he had ordered the boats to sail independently into the harbor, but he recognized there were good reasons for either choice. The boat's crews were quickly taken aboard and the boats themselves were left in the water to trail behind. The sun was well up when they entered the bay and got close enough to shore to see what was going on. The battery seemed intact, but a British flag over a tricolor was flying from the battery's pole. A crowd of townspeople appeared to be menacing the British sailors in the battery, but they could see the Marines, as well as a party of armed sailors guarding the open rear of the battery. As they went close by the merchant brig they had come for, its flag came fluttering down.

Phillips ordered an armed boat crew into a boat to take the brig. As soon as they were on the vessel and had its crew under control, the ship continued toward shore. A couple of mounted men in uniform had ridden up to the crowd menacing the captured battery. One of them pulled out a short carbine and fired an ineffectual shot at the men. The seamen and Marines answered with a volley and a few members of the crowd fell. When another shot came from the crowd, Phillips ordered a gunner's mate, who had been left on the ship, to fire a forward gun at the crowd. The gun roared and the ball hit the ground a few score yards before the mob. The ball bounced right over most of the crowd, but knocked over a file of people in the rear, leaving a few people on the ground. The screaming mob disappeared into the village and Phillips told his men to hold their fire.

Going ashore, he learned from his men the sequence of events. It seemed as the men were marching on the road past the village, a pair of dogs had menaced them. They made such a racket that some villagers came out of their homes. Since the crew had just come up on the battery, they had attacked its unguarded rear on the run. The artillery men had not been able to get to their small arms and either surrendered or ran away directly. However some brave souls in town had opened fire with whatever weapons they had and a half dozen people from the Exeter had been killed and wounded. After some of the snipers had been eliminated, the rest ceased fire.

Braddock was put in command of the defense and men were sent into the village to find whatever military equipment and supplies were available. The gunner was given the order to do as much damage as he could to the guns of the battery. The guns were already loaded, so he maneuvered one around so that its muzzle was inches away from a trunnion on another gun. The men were ordered behind the earthen embankment in front of the battery. The gunner pushed his vent prick down through the touchhole, to make sure the flash had a pathway into the main charge. He pushed a length of slow match down the touchhole.

Covering the area around the touchhole with a heavy damp cloth, to make sure sparks from the match did not prematurely reach the charge, he cut the fuse to the length he wanted and looked around, making sure nobody was unprotected. He himself was close to the embankment, so blowing on his match, he touched it to the match protruding from the breech. As soon as that started burning, he ran up the embankment and dived over. It took a few minutes for the fire to reach the charge, but then the gun went off with an almighty explosion.

The gun slammed back on its trail and came back down, intact. The target gun was torn spinning from its carriage, with an iron trunnion gone and a big divot in the breech. Two other guns in the battery were served in the same manner. Finally, the gun surviving was loaded with a double charge of powder, with a pair of eighteen pound balls down the muzzle. Wooden wedges were jammed in, freezing the balls in place, then earth was pounded into the muzzle.

When finished, again the men were hidden behind the embankment and again the gun was touched off. Again the tremendous explosion and the breech of the gun had burst open.

After examining the carnage, the gunner found one gun that could just possibly be fired again. It still had a bit of a trunnion left. He pulled a hardened steel spike from his pouch and hammered that into the touchhole of the gun just as far as it would go. He struck the spike from the side, breaking it off. When Phillips examined the guns, he could think of no way any of them could be fired again, without a great deal of work first.

The people searching the village had returned. One obvious target for destruction was a ship on the stocks, its frame in the process of being clad. A warehouse had been found, holding such materials as baled raw wool and casks of oil. He had one cask rolled over to the stocks and oil splashed liberally around the hull. His servant, Jones, came running up asking if he could have one of the bales of wool. He could see no earthly use for the material, but had no time to debate. Nodding to the man, he watched as a crew put fire to the hull, setting a blaze that would prove impossible to put out.

The carpenter has discovered a shed filled to capacity with sawed lumber. He had a crew carry away as much of the timber as the men could manage. Finally, the sail maker found a large store of sail cloth in the warehouse and again, as much was salvaged as possible.

The remainder of the material left on shore was also set ablaze, before the ship set sail. As the ship sailed out of the harbor, a troop of cavalry clattered into town. They dismounted and fired a volley, but the balls from the short barreled carbines could not begin to reach the ship.

The ship went back to the former anchorage and located the buoy fastened to the anchor cable. Recovering the anchor, HMS Exeter and her consort set sail to locate the British Channel Fleet.

CHAPTER SEVEN

To the Rescue

Commander John Phillips waited nervously by the lee rail on the quarterdeck of the 64 gun ship of the line, HMS Thunderer. Captain Astor was conversing by the windward rail with the ship's sailing master, the first lieutenant standing by deferentially. Finally, Astor nodded at the lieutenant, who came forward and spoke to the captain, glancing at Phillips as he did so.

The lieutenant came over to Phillips and said, "Sir. The captain will see you in his quarters in a few minutes." The two officers waited by the lee rail for a bit until the captain went below.

A few minutes after the admiral left, the first lieutenant said, "Sir, I think you can go in now."

After being announced by the Royal Marine sentry and entering the captain's office, Phillips waited for him to finish going through the paperwork he had in front of him.

Captain Astor looked up from the reports Phillips had just submitted concerning his recent activities. "I see that you have picked up a prize on your way here. You want to tell me about it?"

Phillips explained the details of the capture, including the quantity of sailcloth he had brought out of the village.

"Excellent, Captain Phillips. I believe you are one of the first to take a French prize. We have a new war, one that we must begin to learn how to prosecute. Thus far, Lord Howe has not been able to bring out the fleet; even with the Impress Service working its hardest.

I understand there is much difficulty finding crews for the ships laid up in ordinary. However, we small fry on the scene shall do the best we can to bring confusion to the enemy."

Phillips wondered, "Sir, what would you have the Exeter doing?"

"Captain, you will be doing the usual small ship duties you might expect on this station. Until we get some more ships, you will be very busy keeping your eye on the various ports in the area, especially Le Havre. We need to know anything you may discover about the naval ships there, especially the line of battle ships. There is much coasting traffic along this coast and I want you to pay attention to that also.

"As you may already know, the roads in this region are in abominable condition, making it difficult to transport goods from where they are produced to the location where they are needed.

Thus, many of the naval stores required for ship building and maintenance are sent by sea."

"If you can interdict that traffic you will cause the French enormous damage, the extent of which will be much more than the value of your own ship. You have already earned your keep with the capture of your prize and the destruction of the battery. Anything more will surely be the icing on the cake."

"Any of that shipping we can disrupt, will be a feather in our cap. I expect to see other sloops and brigs joining us shortly and hopefully more and larger ships. For the moment, I do have an ancillary task for you."

"Recently, a former Army officer and member of the Lords approached the Admiralty with a scheme to incite rebellion along the French channel coast. What I think of the plan is neither here nor there; I just need to tell you that I have orders to facilitate Colonel Lord Henry Fitzhugh, Viscount Bieulieu's mission."

Astor called his sentry. "Private Atkins, please pass the word for the first lieutenant."

The request had barely finished echoing around the ship, when the harried lieutenant appeared at the door.

"Mister Harrison, would you have an officer ask Colonel Fitzhugh to join us on the quarterdeck, please?"

On the quarterdeck, a senior midshipman escorted a tall, aristocratic looking gentleman to the windward rail, where Astor and Phillips waited. Captain Astor introduced the two. "Lord Fitzhugh, please meet Captain Phillips, who will be carrying you aboard his ship to your landing point. Lord Henry, would you acquaint Captain Phillips of your plan?"

"Certainly; a good friend of mine since childhood, is the seigneur of a large estate on the French coast. He was able to get his family away to England before the mob came for him and he was forced to flee. He has since gathered together a force of men who do not care for the new order. His band has been living rough in areas of his estate, where he is well known and is knowledgeable of the terrain."

"In a letter to me he was able to send out by fishing boat, he reports that many of the people have become disillusioned and want a return to the status quo. He says the main problem he faces, is the lack of arms. If he had even a hundred stand of arms, he could arm enough men to capture the local constabulary, where he could find more weapons and arm more men."

"Before my inheritance, I was a lieutenant colonel of my regiment. While I am no longer in the Forces, I do have friends. I have purchased two hundred old muskets and have had them refurbished into working condition. I propose to land them at a point on the coast designated by my friend. I will accompany the weapons on shore and will help my friend organize his troops and give him any military advice that I can."

There were several tons of cargo to be shifted and the master, having already crammed the ship with stores, had to locate new corners to stow the weaponry. Phillips evicted his lieutenant from his cabin and installed the Viscount there. He had offered up his own sleeping cabin, but Lord Fitzhugh demurred, saying he would be aboard for only a few days anyway. Fitzhugh brought on board with him two additional people, one his head gamekeeper and a former Regimental Sergeant Major he had once served with.

Once the problems of stowing the cargo and the new people were resolved, Lieutenant Braddock approached Phillips with a worried look on his face. "Sir, some of the men asked to have access to your sleeping quarters while you were away. The sail maker and his crew wanted to make a few alterations to your accommodations. I gave them permission. If I have done wrong, I most humbly apologize and ask your pardon."

"Well", the bemused captain said, "let us take a look."

Entering, Phillips noticed the bed. This was basically a large wooden box, hanging from the overhead with a line to each corner. The previous captain had had the quarters stripped when he left, including the mattress and bedding, but leaving the empty box frame. With the abrupt departure from port, there had been no chance (or funds) to purchase new bedding, so for the time being, he had been sleeping in a seaman's hammock.

As a boy and young man, he had become used to the article, but after being away from a hammock for a decade, he was finding it difficult to get his body used to it. Now though, there was a mattress in the bed, decorated with blue flowers embroidered on the sun bleached sailcloth. A lot of effort had gone into the project, necessarily on the worker's own time and Phillips was touched. The sail maker was standing by, along with the Marine sentry.

"Men, I am very pleased and I thank you. What in the devil did you make the mattress from and what did you stuff it with?"

The sail maker answered. "Sir, our fore topsail was wore thin, so I made a new one with the canvas we captured. I made a bag with the old topsail and stuffed it with the wool we loaded on the ship, back when we took the brig. A couple of the hands embroidered it. The purser gave us the blankets."

Phillips went back on deck to observe the loading of the cargo. Fitzhugh was also watching, while beside him were his two men. The RSM was still wearing his regimentals and was holding a weapon Phillips was not familiar with. The gamekeeper was clad in green dyed clothing and was holding two long arms of similar design. One weapon held by the gamekeeper was ornately decorated, with silver furniture and a highly figured walnut stock.

The other two weapons seemed to be identical to the ornate piece, except they were fitted with iron furniture and the stocks were of standard grade walnut. Fitzhugh saw him eyeing the weapons and said, "Higgins, show Captain Phillips your rifle, please."

The weapon was a beautiful work of art, perfectly balanced. Fitzhugh explained, "These three are all physically the same. Mine is, however, a little more ornate. They are rifles of course, capable of knocking a man or horse down at three hundred yards. You will note the three rear sight leaves on each weapon. Each is calibrated for a different range; one, two or three hundred yards. The sights not being used would be turned down."

Phillips observed, "Back in the American war, I understand there was trouble with rifles because of the slow speed of loading and the lack of a bayonet?"

"These issues have been addressed, Captain. Sergeant Major, would you demonstrate the method of fixing the bayonet?"

The RSM came to the position of attention, with the weapon's butt plate on the deck and the barrel vertical along his body. His left hand pulled the rifle diagonally across his body, so the muzzle was even with the point of his chin. Holding the weapon with his left hand, he now reached to his side and withdrew a sword-like bayonet from its scabbard and twisted it firmly onto the muzzle. He then came back to the position of attention.

"Would you let the captain examine your rifle, Sergeant Major?"

The RSM came to Port Arms and pushed the weapon out for Phillips to grasp. The weapon was heavier than it looked, probably, Phillips thought, a good ten pounds, perhaps more.

The Viscount said, "We don't want to foul the RSM's weapon, Captain Phillips. Let us fire mine, instead."

"My Lord, it would be better if we waited a few minutes. I need to get the ship under way and discuss some matters with my first lieutenant and master. I will be at your service in a few minutes."

Phillips gave his sailing master the chart for their destination and asked if he had any comments. "Shoal water in the harbor sir, but we should just be able to get in at low tide. We might want the lead going, in case there is a wreck, or uncharted sandbar in the harbor."

"Very well, Mister Avery, Make it so. Would you take us there please?"

With the sails trimmed to the prevailing breeze off their starboard quarter, the sloop sailed sweetly along. After checking with the bosun and Lieutenant Braddock, Phillips left the deck to master's mate Ackroyd and joined the Viscount at the stern, who was looking over the counter at the wake.

"Lord Fitzhugh, would you still wish to tell me about your rifle?"

"Well, I had been discussing some ideas with my gun maker. He had been experimenting with rifled weapons and wished to try out some ideas. I funded some of those and we came up with a finished product. I had been hoping to get Ordnance interested in the matter, but then this present matter popped up. We decided to put the matter on hold until I had more time."

Fitzhugh lifted the flap of a cartridge box hanging from a strap over the Viscount's shoulder and drew out an ordinary appearing paper cartridge. Ordinary, except in the sense of being much smaller than the ordinary Brown Bess musket cartridge. He tore the tail off the cartridge and spilled the powder charge on the deck.

He started to go on, but Phillips raised his hand and said, "Just a moment, my Lord."

Catching the eye of a seaman coiling down a line by the mizzen, he said, "Phelps, would you fetch a swab and get this powder off the deck?"

Fitzhugh apologized, "I'm sorry Captain Phillips. I did not realize I was violating any naval rules."

"We have to be very careful here of fire, Lord Fitzhugh. The problem is being taken care of, though."

"Very well, captain. Would you examine the projectile now?"

Phillips took the remains of the cartridge in his hand and removed the remains of the outer paper covering. Inside, there was a wrapping of very thin paper over two, seemingly separate lead projectiles.

Fitzhugh explained, "We dampen the paper before we wrap the bullets, it shrinks on and when dry loads into the muzzle easier."

Phillips observed, "So you have two bullets coming out the muzzle upon firing. Doubling the chance of hitting your target, I suppose?"

"Not quite Captain. Observe." He pulled the bullets apart and showed them. Each had a conical point and had a similarly shaped conical cavity in its base. "It is difficult to see, but the point of the rear projectile does not quite fit properly into the cavity of the front projectile. The angle of the point on the rear projectile is very slightly larger than the cavity of the forward projectile. The whole assembly is very slightly smaller than the bore of the weapon, making it easy to load. The projectiles, in their paper wrapper, slide easily down the bore. Upon firing, two things happen. The force of the explosion expands the hollow base of the first projectile, forcing the lead to grip the rifling. Then, the first projectile is jammed into the hollow base of the second projectile, also expanding it and jamming the two into one long, heavy bullet."

"How the devil do you make the things, Mold them?"

"No, we tried that, but it was difficult to make perfectly cast bullets. We swage them. A base die is made of hardened steel. A lubricated lead slug is placed in that die. Another steel die is placed over the assembly and a weight is dropped on the whole thing. I happen to be the local magistrate and use our ne'er do wells to handle the heavy work. A day spent forming bullets will make a man think twice before he looks for trouble."

The wardroom steward was sent below to fetch some empty wine bottles. The four men spent the next hour attempting to break floating bottles that had been tossed from the stern of the ship. Then the Marines tried their hand, while finally the armorer was prevailed upon to break out some of the ship's muskets for the crew to practice with. The gamekeeper could almost always break a bottle with his first shot. The Viscount was nearly as good, while the RSM and Phillips trailed.

Two days later, the master informed Phillips the headland behind which the fishing village that was their destination lay would come in sight shortly. Ackroyd was sent below for the Viscount to get his input as to their future actions.

As the wooded headland came into view, Fitzhugh said, "First, we need to come within easy view of the village, flying the old French flag, the 'Fleur de Lys'. We should take our time, approaching the village as close as practical, perhaps closing a fishing boat. After the citizens of the village have noticed us, we can move out seaward, but remain in sight of the headland."

"Sometime after dark, a fire should be lit on the headland. When we spot it, we send a small boat with a few men. This boat should not land near the fire, but some distance away, at a small beach. When it lands, a man should go ashore, while the boat stands off away from the beach. The man ashore will show a blue light and wait for someone to join him. They will decide then their further actions."

Phillips mulled over the plan. "I need to tell you Lord Fitzhugh, that I have only one person on this ship who speaks French fluently and he is a boy, a midshipman whom I would hate to put in a position where he might be taken up for spying. Also, I should say we do not have a 'Fleur de Lys' flag on the ship."

Fitzhugh responded, "I am fluent myself and will go ashore. I also have such a flag in my effects. Needless to say, my friend was not specific as to his actual position. He will probably be with his band somewhere in the forest, but probably has someone in the village to watch out for the 'Fleur de Lys' we will be flying."

"It would be too dangerous to signal us from the village, but any shepherd could light a campfire on the headland without comment. My instructions go no farther than this. I will need to meet the person lighting the fire to find out where we will need to land the weapons. That person will see our boat
approach and be able to meet us on the beach."

Spending much of the day cruising in the bay, with no obvious attention attracted, the Exeter left at nightfall. Again, there was a low overcast and no moon. When it seemed the night was a dark as was possible, the watch on the deck, as well as the deck officer spotted a fire on shore spark into life.

The master reminded Phillips there was no beach near the fire. It was on the top of a vertical cliff that ran down into shoal water. However, there was a tiny beach a half mile away, in a little indent of the cliff and the master thought he recalled a path going up the cliff face. There was also a path of sorts running along the base of the cliff right into town.

The ship cruised offshore of the beach, dropping anchor within good cannon shot of the shore. Braddock gave Mister Withers who was in charge of the jolly boat his instructions.

Viscount Fitzhugh reflected, "Captain, I have reconsidered and decided to take a common musket ashore, to demonstrate my solidarity with them. Could you let me borrow one?"

Phillips called over the Sergeant of Marines and relayed the request. The sergeant in turn ordered a private to divest himself of his equipment and the Sea Pattern Musket he carried. The first lieutenant accepted the gear from him and passed it down into the jolly boat.

Phillips gave the Viscount's weapon and gear to his servant and instructed him to take them to his quarters. After the jolly boat had left, Phillips called Braddock over and ordered him to bring the ship to quarters.

"Mister Braddock, I do not like this situation at all. I would like the ship cleared for action, with guns manned. For now, we will have round shot loaded, but I would like it if we had grape available for reloads; if we need them. The launch should be readied, Ackroyd to command, with the boat gun aboard, ready to assist the jolly boat if needed."

"It should stand by a bit to the south so it will not mask our guns. I also would like a spring on the anchor cable. Our port broadside should bear on the beach where our boat is landing."

This last would entail some trouble, as it called for running a cable via the capstan through a rear port, then forward to the anchor cable itself. A turn of the capstan would turn the long axis of the ship. The ship's broadside could be shifted from one aiming point to another in short order by men heaving at the capstan.

The master had remained by the helm, with his night glass focused on the jolly boat, now nearing the shore. He warned, "Landing party ashore now."

At that moment, there was the blast of a gun on shore, followed by the crackle of musketry. Phillips roared, "Fire on that gun and reload with grape." As the broadside crashed out, three more guns on the beach fired at the jolly boat, which was trying to get off shore. Phillips quietly ordered Braddock to sweep the beach with grape.

The guns continued firing until no further fire from the beach was apparent then he ordered the launch to investigate. From the Exeter, the jolly boat appeared to be dead in the water. The master approached with his night glass extended, "Sir, I can just see men on the beach road. Don't see any guns."

Phillips took the glass, but had a difficult time with it. The image it showed was upside down and hard to decipher. None the less, the order was given to buoy the cable and let slip. The ship would follow the retreating men down the beach path, firing as they sailed.

It was difficult for the fleeing enemy to escape. The ship was faster than they could travel. Some tried to climb the cliff, but a blast of grape soon ended that plan. Some tried to take refuge in the water, but even when hiding underwater a few inches, the grape could often find them.

When the ship finally gave up the chase and returned to the landing beach, the launch was waiting for them. The jolly boat was drawn up on shore. As Ackroyd reported, she had taken much of a charge of grape, killing or wounding half her crew and leaving the boat in a sinking condition.

Ackroyd had beached the jolly boat, giving such aid to its crew that he could, with the launch standing just offshore covering the area with the boat gun. While searching the beach, his men discovered the bodies of Fitzhugh and his men. The bodies had been riddled with the musket caliber grape the French were using in their light field guns.

Phillips oversaw a burial party to lay his dead to their final rest, but decided to leave the French casualties to their own people. One wounded enemy officer was found and brought aboard ship. He had a lot to say. It seemed the M. D'Orleans, the Viscount's friend, had been captured early on and forced to pen letters to Britons who might wish to aid him.

When he had finally refused to write more, he had been summarily executed. The letters written to Fitzhugh and his friends were inspired by the area's radical political leaders for the sole purpose of sabotaging British efforts to bring the war to the continent.

CHAPTER EIGHT

Battle by Land and Sea

It was a blustery fall day when Exeter found the Thunderer, close-hauled to a strong westerly wind. In the absence of instructions from her, Phillips came in astern and followed the battleship. Later that same day, the lookouts spotted a brig, hull down to the west. As she drew nearer, she signaled her number to the liner, which Exeter's new signal midshipman also read.

Mullins reported, "She's gun brig Bulldog, sixteen guns, Sir. Lieutenant Drummond commanding."

"Well, we will no longer be the junior ship on the station", Phillips mused to the master.

Next morning, Lieutenant Braddock, coming up from the wardroom, noticed signal flags flying from the Thunderer, with Exeter's number prominent. With no one from the signal crew on the quarterdeck, the outraged officer screamed for Mullins who was meditating up forward in the heads. The signal yeoman, who had been nattering with one of his friends jumped to his station, read the signal from memory and reported to the first officer, "Signal to Exeter and Bulldog, 'Captains repair on board'."

Phillips had heard the exchange while in his cabin and was now on deck in his new coat and a decent hat, a report on his failed mission with Viscount Fitzhugh under his boat cloak. He ordered, "Get an acknowledgement hoisted and the launch lowered."

The Bulldog with a more alert signal crew had beaten him to the flag by a good five minutes. Phillips climbed the side of the line of battle ship and saluted Captain Astor to the twittering of boatswain's pipes and the stamp of Marines. A rotund lieutenant in a rather ancient uniform was standing beside the captain and Phillips guessed this was the gun brig's captain.

Astor ushered them both to his quarters and his servant put glasses of wine in their hands. While his captains were sampling the wine, Astor looked briefly over Phillip's documents. He expressed his condolences over the death of the Viscount. "You say the French knew about our plans, all along?"

"Yes sir, According to a French officer we captured, the friend of the Viscount was captured early on. He penned those letters to Lord Fitzhugh at the command of the French political officials in this district. When this friend refused to write any more letters, he was executed forthwith."

"Dreadful business. Do you still have the weapons you were to deliver?"

"Yes sir, they were never landed. Apparently the trap was sprung early. Presumably because the Viscount was met by French soldiers, rather than the partisan he expected. It was pure carelessness on their part. We captured four of the French army's field guns, about four pounders. We eliminated their crews with grape. The gun carriages were damaged too badly, so we burned them as well as their limbers. Those horses still alive were sacrificed. The guns were brought aboard ship."

"Well, I am dreadfully sorry for the loss of the Viscount and his people but the success of this mission was never counted upon. Coming to other matters. I would like you to meet Lieutenant Drummond, commanding Bulldog, of sixteen guns." During the ensuing conversation, Phillips learned the Bulldog was fresh out of ordinary and the new officer, Drummond, was right off many years on the beach.

"Gentlemen", Captain offered, "I have just learned from orders delivered to me a few moments ago by Captain Drummond, that I will be the Commodore of this band of Merry Men."

"I have not yet told my first lieutenant, so you will have to wait a bit to view my broad pendant. However, I do want to explain my wishes to you without further delay. Thus far, the French fleet has not honored us by making an appearance. Perhaps they are in the same straits as us, attempting to get old, worn out ships from ordinary and to find trained seamen from wherever they have taken themselves."

"Whatever the reason, it is our duty to make their efforts as difficult as possible. Their coast roads are in deplorable condition and they will find it much easier to transport men, provisions and materiel by coastal shipping rather than by foot or wagon."

"Captain Drummond, you may not know as yet, that Captain Phillips has recently made a pretty penny for himself and his crew by capturing a brig that was hiding in a small bay north of here."

"The brig's captain apparently thought he was safe, since the bay was guarded by a battery of four eighteen pounders. Captain Phillips sent a landing party ashore at the next inlet and his people marched along the coastal road and attacked the battery from the rear. After his party secured the battery, the Exeter entered the bay and her people took the brig and the town, capturing some much needed sailcloth and timber in the process."

"I wish to see actions like this continued. Thus, I am sending the two of you on a cruise, to see what mischief you can get into. You will patrol between Le Havre and Brest, causing as much harm to the enemy as you may. I will expect you back here in two weeks with a report."

Phillips asked Drummond to stop by the Exeter on the way to his own ship. There, he had his servant lay out some wine for his guest. He was no longer embarrassed by his quarters, as the carpenter had finished with his cabinet work and he now had storage space for his clothing and gear. He did need more cabin stores to entertain guests, but that could wait until reaching port. The limited stores he had purchased from the naval outfitter were enough to stave off total embarrassment.

The first lieutenant and master came in with the charts and a council of war begun.

The plan, as it developed, called for the two vessels to sail easterly along the coast, right around the Cotentin Peninsula and on toward Ushant. Generally, the Bulldog would remain as close to shore as practicable, perhaps flying the French tricolor, while the Exeter would remain farther out.

Initially, the plan worked well. The Exeter's lookouts spotted a hull-down sail at seven bells in the forenoon watch. The ship spotted was barque rigged and heading toward a small port at the head of a sheltered bay to the east of the Cotentin Peninsula. The barque was close-hauled to the offshore breeze and it appeared the ship would, with the advantage of her rig, make port without needing to tack.

Exeter steered slightly away to avoid appearing threatening. The Bulldog, making to windward a bit, as if she too was trying to make the same port, appeared innocent as a lamb, with her tri-color flying.

As the Bulldog approached the target, the barque became suspicious and tried to put the wind on her quarter and get out to sea, but the Exeter was already there and now showing her proper colors. The Bulldog came up, with a bone in her teeth and guns bristling, while the barque's master was dithering. Bulldog's tri-color dropped and she hoisted the British Union also.

At that, the prize-to-be let fly her sheets and surrendered. Bulldog's captain went aboard to inspect, as did Mister Braddock of Exeter. Reporting back, Braddock itemized the cargo as sawn timber, tanned hides, shoes and harness; a valuable prize indeed.

To make matters better, she had a mixed crew; some of them, Dutch and Germans, seemed willing to change loyalties and ship under the British flag, instead of the Tri-color.

Leaving Braddock aboard Exeter, Phillips went aboard the prize. Drummond reported he had found six members of the Bonne Citoyenne's crew who were willing to serve in the British Navy in lieu of being sent to the prison hulks, but he hated to leave the men aboard the prize, in case they had a change of heart later and tried to retake the ship.

Phillips thought a moment and said, "Send me three of them and you take the other three. We can then make up a prize crew with people from the Exeter and Bulldog. Do you have anybody to take command of the prize?"

"Well, pondered Drummond, "For navigation officers, I have only my first lieutenant and master's mate, besides myself. But for my sawbones, I have a surgeon's mate, who once served on a slaver as mate. I've had him on the quarterdeck taking sights and I'd warrant him to bring the ship to port safely." "Fine." said Phillips. "I have a good bosun's mate who is a fine seaman and I'll throw in some prime topmen."

"I believe I can furnish the rest of her crew," said Drummond.

The warships began transferring the men and their sea chests, with all being complete by mid watch. At first, the enemy battery fired a round occasionally as a warning, but with the offshore breeze pushing them out to sea, that soon died out. None of the balls had come anywhere near them and Phillips thought their battery commander was just using the occasion as an excuse to exercise his gunners.

Before parting, Phillips met with the new captain of the prize, the former surgeon's mate with the boatswains' mate acting as the second in command. "Before we part, are you gentlemen confident you can make a British port safely?"

Both men agreed they could do so, Phillips addressed Taggart, the prize master. "Mister Taggart, you have your position and copies of our charts. As to seamanship, you will listen carefully to whatever advice your second in command, Mister Montgomery has to impart. Are we understood?"

After again agreeing, Phillips bade them both goodbye and briefly conferred with Drummond before going over the side. "Captain Drummond, I'd like to discomfit that battery ashore that has been potting at us. We will set sail as though leaving and once around the headland, I would like you to come alongside and we will confer."

That evening, the ships came together after the sun dipped below the horizon and Phillips gave his orders. "Before sunrise, I will take a party ashore to deal with that battery. I propose to land on the shore road a mile or so from the battery and march the party along it until we arrive at the location. You will take Bulldog to the bay and demonstrate in front of the battery, taking care to remain out of range."

"You may want to have your remaining boat approach the battery in a threatening manner. You may attempt to make the battery's gunners to believe they might be attacked from your boats. When you hear our attack, at your option, you may give us fire support with all due discretion. I would like it if you would not send any balls past my ears."

With the details out of the way, Phillips took aboard Drummond's first officer, Mister Marshall and some of the Bulldog's landsmen, to fill out the landing party. The party went into the boats, at the start of the middle watch. Four hours later, the oarsmen were resting on their oars just offshore.

With no undue sounds apparent other than the lapping of the surf on the beach, Phillips gave the order to close the beach. Not wanting to make unnecessary noise, he had his landing party go over the side in waist deep water. He savagely remonstrated with a couple of men who thought it appropriate to exclaim loudly about the cold water. When the party got to the road, he put those men at the head of the column so they would have the best chance of being fired upon first.

The party trudged along the road for an hour, before he judged they were closing the battery location. Walking ahead of the party a hundred yards with the malefactors, he thought he heard men talking. When he saw a trail branching from the road toward the sea, he hurried back along the column warning the party they were about to halt.

Sometimes, a column of men halting suddenly, could cause men to jam up close together, with consequent confusion and noise. With a warning, Phillips hoped to prevent that. Mister Marshall had a little French and thought the voices heard came from sentries complaining about their corporal.

There was high ground toward the east and the sun would be a little late in making an appearance, but that did not dissuade a rooster the French troops had, from announcing his presence. Someone's dog, possibly catching a scent, also began barking vigorously.

Phillips had designated Lieutenant Marshall as commander of his reserve force as well as the signal officer charged with signaling the ships. The dozen men of the reserve force would hold back from the initial attack and advance into the fray anywhere the attack seemed to falter.

There were shouts in the enemy camp as men called out epithets to the barking dog. Thinking this confusion was as good a chance as any, Phillips ordered Marshal to ignite the blue light as soon as he heard the party make contact with the enemy. The blue light was a wooden container holding a pyrotechnic mixture that would burn with a brilliant, blue flame. This would warn the ship the attack was starting and hopefully blind the defending soldiers.

As Phillips ordered the men to prime their weapons and advance, Marshall placed the blue light on a large boulder and raised his dark lantern. As the men started to run, one fool fired his musket, starting the dance, so Marshall opened the shutter on the lantern and ignited the blue light.

As cries of alarm came from the French camp, the pyrotechnic became fully alit and a glaring blue light lit up the night. When the attacking party swept through the camp from the rear, many of the erstwhile defenders broke and ran out the front. Some of those who stood and faced the attackers paid the price.

CHAPTER NINE

Securing an Enemy Battery

The attack was over in minutes. Basically, the landing party swept through the emplacement from the rear and the defenders ran out the front, into the forest on either side.

After the initial excitement had subsided, Phillips and Marshall organized a defense all around the encampment. This was a new battery, probably in place for only a few weeks. A wooden causeway laid upon the sand showed where the guns and other heavy gear had been trundled ashore after being unloaded from the transport.

Men searching the shallows at the head of the bay found a swamped barge, abandoned there after the battery had been established. Phillips thought he had perhaps a day before enemy forces began to gather before the installation. He had planned to destroy the guns in the same manner as they had the previous battery, but his boatswain came to him with an idea.

"Sir, I think we can pump out that barge and load those guns on it. I think it will hold them. We could float it out into deep water and sink it. Bore a hole in the bottom and it will sink, right enough, or we could just fire a couple of musket shots through the bottom."

Checking the chart, Phillips noticed there was an area near the mouth of the bay with a depth of ten fathoms or more. He thought that sixty feet of water was enough to prevent the guns from ever being found or raised.

His gunner had some hardened steel spikes in his equipment box. He set to work pounding a spike into the touchhole of each gun, then breaking each brittle spike off. Since the spikes were harder than the surrounding cast iron of the guns themselves, it would be a major job to return them to working order, even if they could be raised.

Men were put to work digging a channel into the beach at the foot of the causeway. His people found some heavy timbers laid into the parapet of the battery. The prisoners, upon being questioned, reported they had originally made up the big tripod that had been used to hoist the weapons from the barge.

While his men were busy retrieving them, a delegation of civilians came down to the beach. Midshipman Mullins was brought ashore to speak to them. He reported, "Sir, the soldiers appropriated their oxen to use for rations. They want the cattle that are still alive back."

His bosun had already reported they needed some draft animals to move the guns. Phillips knew there were half a dozen bullocks in a pen in the camp, but had no notion of working them. He told Mullins the locals could have the cattle, if they could get them to move the guns onto the barge.

The locals were concerned because the cattle had not been fed and would be weak from hunger, so he ordered a hundred pounds of biscuit brought ashore and given to the cattle. Once the first of the suspicious bullocks sampled the strange biscuit, the rest went after it like starving wolves.

While the trench was being excavated, another party went to the marsh where the barge had been abandoned. Its gunnels were about even with the top of the water, but a portable pump was brought to the site and men sent to work pumping.

At first, it seemed water slopped over the gunnels back into the boat as fast as it was removed, but after some men set to work baling with buckets also, the crew started making some headway. The water level in the barge soon began to drop rapidly. Presently, it was necessary to scoop out the foot of mud that filled the bottom of the boat.

The boat finally began to float. Its oars could not be found, so the Exeter's launch tied onto it and towed it to the dugout portion of the causeway where it was manhandled into position. The big twelve pounder cannons were on carriages, so locals quickly hooked two span of oxen to a gun and hauled it to the tripod, which had been assembled so it straddled the trench. Then, the oxen were brought around to the cable running to the big block at the apex of the tripod. The last pair of oxen was hooked on and all were set to pull. With six animals pulling, the big gun slowly lifted off its carriage and violently swung out over the barge underneath.

The animals were slowly backed until the gun settled into the barge. Crew members pushed the now empty carriage away and the cattle were led around to bring another gun around.

By the time all the guns were on the barge, it had very little freeboard. The gunnels were within inches of the water. After the locals were told they could take the cattle and anything else they wanted from the battery, they swarmed over it like ants, hauling away anything they could carry.

While they were doing this, seamen were tearing up the causeway, piling up the wood under the tripod. Adding anything else that was flammable, including the empty gun carriages, a puncheon of oil found in the cook shack was broached and the fluid spread liberally over the pile. Lieutenant Marshall took a spare blue light and placed it under the oil soaked material.

The bagged powder charges from the magazine were removed and sent aboard both Bulldog and Exeter. This powder could be re-bagged and used for practice ammunition in the future, without having to account for it.

When the incendiaries under the pyre were lit, the blue flames flashed through the pile of material and it was fully engulfed in a moment. Phillips had warned the locals that troops could be expected to arrive at any moment, so they took their spoils and left.

With the locals gone, Phillips ordered the launch to tow the barge into the bay. He pointed out the area he wanted to sink the boat to the coxswain. He advised him to have his men row easy, since it would be easy for water to slop over into the boat and sink it. He made sure the cox'n had a sharp axe with him to cut the line, since if the barge went down it was liable to take the launch with it.

The crew of the launch with some effort got the barge moving. The carpenter went along in the launch with an auger, but it was not necessary. The barge travelled safely enough in the calm water of the bay, but as soon as they reached open water, the sea began slopping over into the barge. The cox'n immediately started chopping at the cable with the axe and just as it parted, the barge's gunnels dipped below the surface and down it went. The cox'n let down a lead line to measure the depth at that point. Seven fathoms, over forty feet deep.

Phillips doubted any divers in the area would be able to descend to that depth and get a line on any of the guns. That would be if they knew where to find them. Phillips could see no sign of the locals. He was sure that none of them had seen the weapons sink. For all the enemy knew, maybe he had loaded the guns aboard ship and taken them away.

CHAPTER TEN

Fleur d'Orleans

Now, it was time to get away from the coast, before the wind shifted and pinned them there. Little Bulldog was first out of the harbor, signaling the way clear. Exeter weighed her anchor and sailed out into the sea with the offshore breeze. As the got out past the headland, Bulldog hoisted 'Enemy in sight', just as their own lookout shouted, "Sail off the starboard bow. Big corvette or maybe a frigate."

A frigate it was, twenty eight guns in total. The British vessels would be taking a big chance were they to try to engage that ship. Her scantlings were much heavier than those of Exeter or Bulldog and her guns were probably larger. Phillips guessed twelve pounders. Exeter and Bulldog carried sixes, although Bulldog also carried a few 32 pounder carronades in forward and aft gun positions.

The frigate was heading straight toward the two British craft. She was now beating against the wind, just able to maintain her course, while Exeter and Bulldog were sailing large. In the enclosed waters, the pair would have to proceed past the broadsides of the frigate, not an appetizing choice. Phillips ordered the signal hoisted, 'Form line astern'.

Bulldog backed her main topsail, slowing to let Exeter pull ahead. As the three ships converged, he told the master to handle the ship, so he could deal with the guns. He said, "I want you to swing us across her bows, so we can rake her." Trusting that Drummond would follow him, he waited. As the frigate came up to them, her guns bristling, she could not fire yet, as she was bows on to Exeter. Phillips guessed she thought Exeter would try to slip by on the frigates starboard side and hoped to blow her to perdition with her broadside. Instead Avery turned the ship to starboard. Phillips ordered loudly, "When your gun bears, fire."

He agonized for an instant that when he said the word 'fire', some blockhead might yank his lanyard immediately, but there was only quiet. The frigate's yards started to swing around to match the sloop's turn, but Exeter beat them to it. As her bow guns started to bear, they began to go off, one by one, the six pound iron balls ripping through the thin scantlings at the frigate's bow and travelled the length of the ship, tearing and rending men, ship and equipment.

The enemy fired a broadside at Exeter, all her port side guns going off more or less at once, but much of it was wasted, many of the guns not bearing on their target. Looking back, he saw Bulldog had not been able to follow him around, holding on instead to cross the enemy's stern, going right on past the now empty enemy guns. She took the opportunity to salute those impotent guns with her broadside.

Her six pounders did their share of damage, on top of the havoc the frigate had received from Exeter, but the carronades were especially devastating at such close range.

Bulldog's petty officers harried the gun crews to hurry the reload, and most of the guns held a charge by the time the gunbrig rounded the frigate's stern.

While savaging the enemy's quarter with her broadside, one of her little six pound balls damaged the frigate's sternpost and her rudder became jammed.

The frigate now being unable to steer, Exeter was able to take station across the bow of the frigate, pounding her with her guns, the shot again travelling the whole length of the ship. The Bulldog laid off the frigate's quarter, smashing her after parts and preventing repair parties from mending the rudder.

Only the aftermost guns on the enemy's port side could reach the brig and those guns were soon put out of action. The loads of grape from the carronades were especially effective in reducing the numbers of enemy crew upon the frigate's deck. Soon the frigate's bowsprit was shot away and then down came her fore topmast. When the whole foremast then fell, the action was nearly over.

Bulldog, still astern, began using grape and canister in all her guns and was now raining a storm of deadly death into the ship. After a final blast cleared the enemy quarterdeck, her flag came hesitantly down.

Phillips roared 'Cease Fire" and after a couple of extra individual crashes, the carnage ended. He looked at Bulldog. Her mizzen was dangerously askew and blood was running from the scuppers. Exeter herself had men sprawled on the deck, dead or wounded and a twelve pound ball had dangerously weakened the foremast.

Much of the rigging had been damaged and the larboard shrouds for the mainmast had been badly damaged. He looked over the side; the launch which had been towing was still afloat. His cox'n was also still alive. Mister Braddock came up the hatchway with a bandaged arm, the remaining pieces of his shirt a mass of gore.

"Mister Ackroyd", Phillips shouted to his signal officer. "Please take some seamen and the Marines and go over to the frigate and take possession. Take the boat crew aboard with you if necessary." He sent Braddock below, again.

Hours of intense labor followed as the three ships were repaired enough to make them barely seaworthy. The crew of the frigate had been hurriedly run below, with boat guns aimed at the hatches. The foremast of the Exeter, as well as the mizzen of Bulldog had to be 'fished'. Lengths of timber were lashed tightly to the masts and the bindings twisted taught. The standing rigging; stays and shrouds, had to be repaired or renewed.

The captured frigate needed to have a jury bowsprit and foremast rigged. The wounded crewmembers of Bulldog were suffering, as they had no doctor aboard. Midshipman Mullins found the captured prize, 'Fleur d'Orleans', had two surgeons mates aboard, in addition to her surgeon, so he ordered one of those mates to report aboard Bulldog, to see what he could do. With all the repairs they were able to perform with their men and materials, the little fleet set sail for Plymouth.

Closing the English coast, they fell in with a '74 gun liner, also destined there. Her captain was so impressed with their feat that he loaned a hundred men, parceled among the three ships.

The "Fleur d'Orleans' got the largest share since she had only a tiny prize crew aboard and a large number of enemy prisoners not at all happy about going into the hulks. Upon reaching port Phillips and Drummond were summoned immediately to the presence of the elated Vice Admiral Cosby.

That gentlemen, after first insisting upon a shot by shot commentary of the action, then ordered them into a post-chaise and sent them into London with a packet to take to the Admiralty. Cosby assured the captain's promotions were probable for both Drummond and Phillips, if his recommendation carried any weight. Perhaps also for their first officers.

Reaching London, Phillips met with Admiral Howe, who praised his enterprise and initiative and was then sent to the waiting room to await orders. After an hour's wait, an ancient lieutenant hobbled up to him on his wooden leg and handed him a packet.

The packet contained a commission appointing him to the command of "Vigorous', a thirty two gunned frigate, now coming out of ordinary in Plymouth. With this commission, he was now a post captain, entitled to wear his swab on his right shoulder instead of the left.

Eventually, with the passage of time, he would be an admiral; should he live that long, of course.

He found he was authorized to take aboard the crew of Exeter, that ship being taken out of service for a much needed survey and repairs. He would be on his own however to fill out the remainder of his crew. He was pleased to find the first prize he had taken had been adjudicated and he now possessed a well filled purse.

It was true that most of the money he was handed was paper currency, which was taking the place of much of the specie throughout Britain but at least he could now afford cabin stores. With his new riches, he was concerned about highwaymen, so stopped by a gun maker and bought a pair of pistols.

He purchased an inside seat on the mail coach, but since the weather was fine and a female passenger inside seemed a twin of the one he had traveled to Portsmouth with weeks earlier, he elected to ride on top with the driver.

His sea chest was loaded up on the coach, but he needed to carry on his person the rifle the viscount had left for him to look after. A cursory search had failed to locate a relative he could delegate the weapon to.

The driver eyed his weapon and his heavy coat pockets. "Always glad to have a well-armed gentleman aboard sir, but you won't have to use the guns this trip. With the hot press the navy has out, all the highwaymen are running for cover."

Halfway to Portsmouth, Phillips realized he had better change to the insignia of a post captain rather than that a mere commander. He removed his coat and switched his epaulette from the left shoulder to the right. Now he was correct.

CHAPTER ELEVEN

HMS Vigorous

In Portsmouth, Phillips first went to the naval outfitter he had obtained his provisions from earlier and made arrangements for cabin stores and other necessities. They were able to tell him right where the ship was anchored. He hired a wherry to take him out to the Vigorous. He was challenged properly by the anchor watch and was met by the carpenter and bosun.

These worthies said the ship had recently been pulled from the mud berth she had rested in for the past decade and had her new copper installed, before being towed out into the harbor. Just to make matters official, Phillips read himself in to the few men aboard.

Deciding his first need was to get some men, he hired a boat to take him to the receiving ship. An elderly lieutenant commanded the ship itself, but the hands on board that he needed were under the control of an officer of the Impress Service. This man agreed to furnish him with one hundred thirty men, supposedly from his old crew on the Exeter, but when they were brought up on deck, he found most were old, decrepit, lame or ruptured. None of them he had ever seen before.

Tearing Howe's order from the man's hand, Phillips made for the entry port without further ceremony. The lieutenant followed, protesting he needed the order in order to send him his men.

Phillips answered, "The men you are offering me are not my men. I see that I need to see the Port Admiral to obtain my people."

Admitting the possibility of a mistake, the officer agreed to allow Phillips to search the ship for his crewmen. After a half hour of searching and finding nobody he recognized, he heard a voice, "Captain Phillips, sir."

Turning, he saw one of his old surgeon's loblolly boys, a ruptured former topman.

"Sir, I know where your men are." After questioning the man, he discovered his seamen were ashore in a warehouse, guarded by a detachment of militia. The Impress officer was making extra money selling able seamen to desperate captains. Loosening the pistols in his pockets, he ordered the man, "Come with me."

His hired boat had left, but a ship's boat transporting a midshipman from a nearby '74 had just hooked on at a larboard entry port. He politely asked the youngster if he could borrow the boat to carry him to the shore. The mid had been given strict instructions to let none of the boat crew out of his sight, but on the other hand, this was a godlike post captain with a reasonable request. Inspirationally, he offered, "Sir, I'd be glad to transport you ashore." On the way ashore, the loblolly boy pointed out the warehouse his men were housed in.

"Sir, all the able bodied seamen are housed here. That Impress Service officer sells 'em to any ship that will pay. All the sick, lame and ruptured, as well as the quota men are housed on the receiving ship to palm off on ships that can't or won't pay.

Straining his brain, Phillips finally remembered the man's name. "Harkins, what about you. I know you are ruptured, but I remember you as a mighty valuable man. You certainly are not required to go back to sea, but I'd be glad to have you if you want."

By the time the boat reached the row of warehouses on shore, it was established Harkins would like to go to sea with his captain. He had earned some prize money on the last voyage and the prospects of earning more seemed excellent. The work he did as loblolly boy was light compared with what he might need to do ashore.

On the beach, they climbed the stone steps to the warehouse, finding it locked with armed sentries patrolling their posts on all sides of the building. A group of soldiers off duty were gathered around a fire in from of the warehouse, with a cornet of about sixteen years seemingly in charge.

He came forward and saluted, awestruck at Phillips uniform.

Phillips was not cognizant of the boy's rank or uniform himself, so merely said, "Sir, I need to retrieve some of my men who I understand are in that warehouse under your care."

"Sir", offered the lad, "Those are Lieutenant Hanford's men and can't be released without an order from him."

"Lad, as you see, I am of superior rank to your Lieutenant Hanford and besides I carry an order from Vice Admiral Howe for these men. I hope you are not going to try to prevent me from collecting them."

The Cornet decided the matter was too far above his position for him to reconcile, so ordered a soldier to take him to his captain. The captain, even more impressed with the order from Howe than the cornet had been, ordered a servant to have horses brought up and told Phillips the colonel was at a party at the George Inn and he would take him there himself.

Now, Phillips had ridden before, but not well and not often. He clambered aboard though and followed the officer. The captain, recognizing the naval officer's lack of confidence, kept to a walk.

They reined in at an imposing inn and entered. Inside were military officers of the army and navy. Among the party was a gaudily uniformed militia colonel dripping with gold lace. The captain approached him and explained. The colonel said, "Order from Admiral Howe, you say? Let us see."

They approached an elderly white haired naval officer seated on the side and Phillips saw with a shock it was Vice Admiral Peter Parker, himself, the port admiral. The man had given him his step to commander a few months before. Now he would have to explain why he couldn't man his new ship. His heart seemed to have dropped to the pit of his stomach.

The colonel asked Parker to examine the order to see if it was genuine and Parker took it and expostulated, "This order is from Lord Howe himself. I recognize his writing. I served with him before. What seems to be the problem?"

Phillips explained the situation to the admiral, about the men being imprisoned in a warehouse and sold to ship captains. Parker beckoned his flag lieutenant who was occupied with chatting up a likely looking young lady. He hurried over and Parker scribbled a note, telling him to take it to a senior post captain drinking port at a table with friends.

When the captain came over, Howe said, "Hardy, I want you to take a file of Marines to the receiving ship and bring back the Impress Service officer commanding there. I want to see him first thing in the morning. Then, I want you to delegate one of your officers to take temporary charge of the guard around the warehouse Captain Phillips will direct you to."

"The men they will be guarding will be proper seamen of the Royal navy and are to be treated decently. Rations will be issued and they will be entered on the books to be paid at their proper rate."

When the officer left, Parker questioned the colonel. "How did the Impress Service office come to engage your men?"

"Well, sir, he is paying us. A shilling per prisoner a week for the guard, he furnishes rations. We thought it a reasonable fee."

"My Marines will take over from your men. I will have them out of that warehouse tomorrow."

The captain with the horses having left, Parker gave Phillips a ride back to the warehouse in his carriage. The militia troops there were forming up to leave. A Lieutenant of Marines had already reported with a party and had taken over the guard. Nobody knew where the key to the lock on the door was located so Parker ordered it to be knocked off.

He went inside the dark building and spoke to the excited sailors gathered there. He assured them he was ashamed that decent British sailors had been treated in such a manner and those responsible would be handled in the appropriate manner. He asked the men to bear with their hardships for a few more hours until matters could be rectified.

Admiral Parker told Phillips, "I remember giving you Exeter. I was worried you were too inexperienced, but you proved me wrong. Now you are a post captain, commanding a fine frigate. What can I do for you?"

"Well sir, I have a ship, but no crew. Admiral Howe said I could have the crew off the Exeter, but I'm going to need more people to bring a thirty two gun frigate up to strength."

"You are certainly entitled to your men. You may have what men you need to bring your ship up to full strength. How about officers. What do you need there?"

"I have no lieutenants, no master or surgeon. No purser either. I do have a gunner, bosun and cook on board."

"The admiral thought, "I have lieutenants coming out of my ears. The trouble is, many haven't worked in a decade and may have forgotten everything they ever knew. I'll see what my staff can find. Need any mids?"

"Yes sir, senior ones if at all possible, to command gun sections and serve on the quarterdeck."

"Well, find some people you know in this mess and sort out the people you need for your ship.

Captains have been begging me for men for weeks and lo and behold, I find half a thousand in one warehouse. Captains will be swarming here tomorrow morning to take their pick, so don't tarry."

When Admiral Parker left in his gig, Harkins appeared from where ever he had been hiding. Phillips ordered the man to enter the warehouse and call out for the Exeter's to come forward, adding, "We'll need more people to man our next ship, the Vigorous. Anyone wanting to join us should come out to talk to me."

As soon as the word started being passed, men, most being former Exeter's, began crowding around. One young man he saw in the rear was the French speaking mid, Mister Mullins. Phillips asked the lad what he was doing among the seamen. The boy answered, "I went into town after the ship paid off and the press caught me. I tried to tell them I was a midshipman, but that Impress Service lieutenant said since I didn't have a ship anymore, I wasn't a mid either. They put me with the men.

"Well, you're a mid now, if you want to sail with me aboard the Vigorous."

"Oh yes sir."

"First things first. Where's your kit?"

It's at the inn, sir. "But the Impress people took all my money, so now I can't pay my bill."

"How much did they take? Where is your inn?"

The boy pointed across the square at a shabby posting inn. "I had a pound note, a guinea and a pair of sixpence, sir."

"Do you think you might have a pen and ink in your kit? "

"Yes sir, if the landlord will let me take it without paying my bill", he said doubtfully.

Phillips pulled a pair of pound notes and a few shillings from his purse. Handing them to the boy, he asked, "Do you think that will pay your bill?"

"Yes sir, more than enough."

"Very well, hurry there, fast as you like, then come back. I want you to make some lists for me. Tomorrow, I'll try to find an officer who can accompany you to a magistrate, where you will file proper charges against the men who robbed you. Would you recognize them again?"

"Yes sir, they took money from some of the other men, too."

When Midshipman Mullins returned, he sat him down with a length of scrap board on his lap and bade him start listing the individual men and the proposed ratings. As each man appeared before Phillips, he was asked his name and rate. Whenever he realized he needed a man who was not available from his Exeter people, he had trusted hands from the already selected people go back into the crowd to search for somebody who could fill that rate. It was a strange way to man a ship, but at least he had men.

One of his newly rated bosun's mates sidled up to him. "Sir, is it true our new ship is empty? No hammocks or rations?"

"That's right, Atkins. In the morning, we'll start to draw what we need, but for now, we'll have to live rough."

"Sir, there's some supplies in that warehouse. Bagged biscuit for one. That's what we've been eating. And we've all been issued hammocks too, though we were told we'd have to give 'em back when we were sent to a ship."

"Atkins, if there is no officer from the impress service here in the morning to return your issue to, you will have to bring the hammocks with you. You men certainly don't want to lose the King's property now, would you? Better have some men carry some of that bagged biscuit. I don't know what rations we have on the ship."

"Nosir, I'll pass the word."

The list of crew was a mess when they finished. Names had been crossed out, new ones added in the margins, ink blots, et cetera. This jogged his memory. He shouted out, "Is there a man here that can write a fair hand? Maybe a former captain's clerk?"

A frail looking middle aged man hesitantly came forward. Phillips could not understand how he came about to be in that gathering. All the others were fit, strong looking and confident seamen. "Clark, sir, Captain's clerk aboard Indomitable."

Clark was handed pen and paper and ordered to make a fair copy of the scribbled mass of papers Phillips handed him. He wrote quickly and accurately, his handwriting was easy to read. "Clark, would you like to sign on as captain's clerk?"

When he agreed, Phillips ordered him to add his name and new rate to the roster. Then he had him write out an order to the cook onboard the Vigorous, telling him two hundred fifty men would be arriving shortly and to arrange to draw provisions for them. Signing the note, he handed the clerk some coins and told him to attempt to hire a shore boat to take him out to the ship.

CHAPTER TWELVE

Getting a Crew

Dawn had come to the harbor and Phillips was still standing on the quay, when a one horse chaise clattered onto the stone pavement and halted. The chaise lifted on its springs, when the ponderous post captain removed his twenty stone weight from the seat. The man had indeed apparently partied well and was in a cheerful mood when he walked up to Phillips. Looking around, he said, "Johnson here, Ariel. Where the devil did you get all these seamen? Want to trade? I need a dozen good topmen."

Thinking quickly, Phillips said, "Captain, my name is Phillips, Vigorous. These men are spoken for, but there are plenty more where I got these, waiting to be entered on a ship's books. You loan me a couple of boats to take these men to my ship and I'll introduce you to the man in charge. Right now, I am in a bind, since I haven't drawn my boats yet."

Captain Johnson looked at the seamen wonderingly and said, "Phillips, you get me some topmen and I'll row you to Halifax." He pointed to a launch thrashing up to the quay. The boat hooked onto the quay and Johnson addressed the young mid in the stern. "Mister Halliday, you will please take as many of these men as you can put in your boat and take them to that fifth rate you see. Deliver them to Vigorous, except for a boat's crew. Then go to the Ariel. Report to the officer of the deck and tell him I need the cutter. The boats crew you brought will man it. Then return here. The possibility exists that I may be bringing some men back."

After the boat left, Phillips led Johnson over to the warehouse. The Marine lieutenant had rebuilt the fire left by the militia and was warming the seat of his breeches in the cold air of the early morning harbor shore. The door of the warehouse was open and men were trying to spill out, but the Marines held them back with difficulty. Phillips led Johnson to the officer and said, "Lieutenant, Captain Johnson here needs some men. Any objection if he looks them over?"

"Be my guest, sir. Take the whole lot if you want."

The two captains walked over to the milling throng, held at bay by the bayonets of the Marines. After studying them for a while, he pointed at one burly middle aged man. "Ripley, is that you?"

The man came over, knuckling his forehead. "Ben Ripley, Captain Johnson. Captain of the maintop on my last ship, the Illustrious."

"We served together on the American station years ago, did we not?"

"Aye sir; that we did. You need some good hands sir; we have some that would be proud to sail with you."

Johnson walked among the men, questioning and selecting hands. When he finished, he asked the Marine officer, "What do I need to do to take delivery?"

"Sir, Just a note saying you are taking the men aboard your ship for duty. List their names and sign. That would do it, sir."

As he scribbled on the paper, Johnson said, "Captains in this port have been sweating blood, trying to find seamen, including myself. Then you just walk up and steer me to as many as a man could ask for. I owe you sir."

"I am glad you got some men, Captain Johnson. I appreciate your help transporting my men to my ship. We don't have our ship's boats yet. Did you get as many topmen as you wished?"

"Got more. Twenty altogether. I'll be over complement if I don't get rid of some. I'll probably let my sawbones discharge some of my 'sick, lame and lazy'.

The morning was well advanced when the last of the men came aboard. When that confusion ended, a shore boat came alongside, carrying a pair of lieutenants. He had no sooner got them below in his cabin, each with a glass of wine, when he heard another boat being challenged.

Hearing the 'Aye, Aye', signifying an officer was aboard, he went back on deck. This boat carried another lieutenant, as well as Mister Avery, the former sailing master of the Exeter. The lieutenant carried a note from Admiral Parker's flag lieutenant, indicating he was sending him three officers, along with Mister Avery, hoping all would be suitable.

Another boat approached, holding a pair of grown men, with a herd of boys of varying ages on board, apparently would-be midshipmen. Two boys were mere children, but four were of a more useful age. Handing the boys over to Mullins, he addressed the adults. One proved to be the surgeon and the other the purser. With a full ship's company, now the main effort was to get it working efficiently. His new lieutenants had already sorted themselves out as to their commissioning dates.

The master and first officer (the senior lieutenant) set out to bring order out of chaos. The second officer was put in charge of the deck, while Phillips gave a signed requisition and some money to the third and ordered him to hire a shore boat to take to the boat pond ashore and try to obtain some ship's boats.

"Better take a boat's crew with you." he advised. The purser likewise was sent ashore to obtain ship's stores. Beer was especially needed. The men could rightfully expect to be issued a gallon each and every day and after their travails lately, he hated to disappoint them.

The third lieutenant soon appeared back alongside in a ship's launch, towing a jolly boat behind. The shore boat was paid off and the new first lieutenant told off a crew for the jolly boat. Filling the boat with as many extra hands as possible, it set out for the boat pond and brought back another boat. Successive trips brought back all the boats they had been allotted.

Now it was time for the provisions. Previously arranged barges came alongside with barrels of salt pork and beef. Others carried bags of biscuit and dried peas, bales of sailcloth and hammocks. Casks of sauerkraut and vinegar were brought aboard, along with the kegs of beer. Butter and oatmeal, raisins and suet, all came aboard.

Big barges laden with the huge tuns of fresh water came along side. Empty water barrels were stowed right down in the hull and the water was pumped from the barge down through the hatches into the lower tiers, before the bungs were tamped home. The men were very interested when the rum came aboard. They knew they would not be issued any in home waters as long as the beer held out, but there was always hope for the future.

There was both an advantage and a disadvantage to the use of beer. To save expense, brewers tended to skimp on malt, ensuring a very low alcoholic content. However, the limited alcohol caused the brew to spoil rapidly, which required the much more valued rum to be issued in its place.

The beer brought aboard the Vigorous was mainly just hops flavored water, so the men knew they would soon be drinking rum. Unless, of course, they were sent to the Mediterranean, where wine was often issued.

With the provisioning of the ship well in hand, the ship itself got much needed attention. Topmasts and yards were floated out behind the boats and highly skilled seamen began putting everything together. Standing rigging was first attended to, then the running gear. Stays and shrouds received their attention, then it was time to bend on the sails. After the yards were crossed, the bundles of flaxen canvas were sent aloft. Installed and furled; the ship was almost ready to sail. First though, she needed to receive her *raison d'etre*.

The captain put the ship's crew and capstan to work, hauling up the heavy anchor. She tested her wings, moving to the ordnance wharf. There she first loaded the wooden gun carriages, then the eighteen pounder guns were swung aboard, each being lowered from the yard right onto its carriage.

Four gun ports, two up forward and two aft, were filled with 36 pounder carronades. These guns, shorter and lighter than the standard long eighteen pounder guns, fired the much heavier standard round ball or grape load as used in the 36 pound long gun, but with a greatly reduced powder charge. This enabled the guns to be cast with less iron in the breech area. Coupled with the shortened barrel, this made a great saving of weight.

Phillips had never had experience with such weapons and discussed the matter with the ordnance officer who came aboard to insure they were installed correctly. He explained the rule now was to issue 32 pounder guns to those frigates that could handle them.

In this case, there were some 36 pounders on hand and it was thought they might be tried out on Vigorous as an experiment.

Few ships could withstand the impact of thirty six pounds of iron flying at hundreds of feet per second. The carronades were mainly useless at longer ranges, but at close range, they were deadly. The grapeshot loads would prove especially dangerous fired at personnel or rigging, much like a greatly enlarged shotgun.

The heavy projectiles, eighteen and thirty six pound iron balls, as well as grape and canister shot assemblies were carried aboard with much effort and struck below. Bar shot was also brought aboard to be used to fire into the masts and rigging of enemy ships.

The gunner and his mates went around each gun, checking to make sure the gun could not come loose in a heavy sea and the gun tackle was secure. Few things were more dangerous than a runaway gun on a rolling or pitching deck.

When the gunner, as well as the first lieutenant, was satisfied with the armament, the ship moved out in the harbor. Away from other shipping, the powder hoy came creeping out, propelled by long sweeps, resembling from afar, a large water beetle. All flames aboard ship were extinguished. All crew on deck were in their bare feet and water was dashed liberally on the deck.

Swabs and buckets of seawater were placed around the deck, so any spilled powder could be swiftly be mopped up. The gunner's crew was prepared to stow the casks of gunpowder in the powder room, where no ferrous metals were permitted. Even the metal bands on the powder casks were either copper or brass so no spark could possibly be struck.

When the job was finished and the 'Danger.' flag lowered, the third officer, acting as ship signal officer, reported the flag had hoisted the signal, 'Captain, repair on board'. Since Vigorous' number had been hoisted with the signal, Phillips knew the signal was directed at him.

Gathering some last minute reports he had spent half the preceding evening preparing, he dropped into the boat his premier had ready for him. At the flagship, the flag captain told him it was the Med for him. He was to carry dispatches to the Mediterranean and to report to Lord Hood, commanding off the Mediterranean coast of France. He was permitted to make a brief stop at

Gibraltar, to see If there was any news there of Hood's actual location. If Admiral Hood was not present, he should use his best efforts to find his fleet. If all else failed, he should locate Ambassador Hammond, probably in Naples, where he was attached to the court of King Ferdinand and deliver the pouch addressed to him. After fulfilling his orders, the Vigorous would come under the command of Hood.

"Very well sir. Should I depart immediately, or should I stay and make my manners with the admiral?"

"Admiral Parker is in London now. In the pouch that came early today, it was emphasized the Importance of delivery as soon as possible. You are required to sail as soon as the state of your ship and the wind and tide permits. We have learned by reports from agents that some French cities are revolting from the excesses of the Directory. Marseille and Toulon are especially mentioned. It is desired to get this information into Lord Hood's hands as soon as possible."

Phillips left the flag and told his coxswain to get them back to Vigorous immediately. Phillips noticed a naval transport, an old frigate near the end of her days, stripped of her guns and commanded by a lieutenant, pulling away. His mind full of the implications of sailing to a destination he had never been to before, he paid no attention. Probably a last minute delivery of purser's supplies.

He clambered aboard the Vigorous to the twittering of boatswain's pipes and lifted his hat in salute to the quarterdeck. The deck officer, seeing him distracted, moved away after lifting his own hat, but the first lieutenant, being made of sterner material intercepted him and said, "Sir, the arms have come aboard and I had them struck below."

"Struck what below, Mister Burns?"

"Muskets sir, two hundred of them, with ammunition and accoutrements."

"I know of no muskets, Mister Burns. Show them to me."

The lieutenant led him below, where the captain of the hold was busy with his party jamming pieces of firewood being used as dunnage between the crates of muskets and other cargo stowed there to prevent it from shifting. "The gunner has the ammunition", reported Lieutenant Burns. Carefully lettered text on one box, now crossed out, stated it was the property of Colonel the Lord Viscount Fitzhugh of HMS Exeter. A later paper label tacked onto the wood crate said, 'Forward to HMS Vigorous, Captain Phillips'.

Phillips recalled after being unable to find Fitzhugh's heir, he had simply left the muskets on board the Exeter when the ship paid off. He assumed the Royal Navy would assume custody and send the arms to their proper destination. Instead, the ever efficient service had forwarded the weapons on to him in his new command.

He had assumed the muskets, being cast off Army weapons of little value, if charged to him, probably would not cost him a large sum. He had held on to Fitzhugh's rifle, which he thought was worth a good deal and had better be properly safeguarded. Shaking his head, he told Burns he had learned what he needed and went to the gunner to see about the ammunition.

Mister Hodges advised him the musket ammunition, although being made for the Army's Land Pattern muskets, was identical to the ammunition carried for the Sea Service muskets aboard ship and could be used in them. The Army muskets could be used also, but were really not needed since the ship already carried all such weapons she could use.

Deciding the musket problem was one he need not concern himself over right away, he went to Lieutenant Burns to discuss the appearance of the ship and exercising the crew in sail and gun drill.

CHAPTER THIRTEEN

Bad Food

On the voyage to Gibraltar, Captain Phillips had the opportunity to thoroughly work his ship up and determine what departments needed work. He soon discovered his Premier, Lieutenant Burns, was an exceptionally capable officer and seaman. He found he need have no qualms about assigning any duty to the officer.

The second office, Lieutenant Harkins seemed to be an average quality officer such as you might find in wardrooms around the fleet by the gross. He would set about any task given him and do his best, but it might sometimes be necessary to keep a wary eye on the man. Harkins was found to sometimes set about matters in which he had little knowledge or skill.

Mister Granger, the third, was a reticent young man, seldom venturing any opinions of his own. His commissioning date indicated this was his first cruise as an officer. Phillips had to wonder how the shy young man had gained his promotion but there was no harm in the lad. He could see the officer would need as much practical experience as could be given him.

No sightings of enemy warships occurred on this leg of the journey, although they did sight a large schooner. They never were close enough to identify her. When first seen, she was heading for the Channel and could be heading for either a British or French port, perhaps even a Dutch, German or Baltic harbor. In the event though, she headed west, as close to the eye of the wind as she could sail, which was several points closer than Vigorous could handle.

As the quarterdeck crew watched her disappear over the horizon, there was speculation as to her origin. Some though a French vessel from the sugar islands in the Caribbean. Others thought a neutral Yankee who was merely attempting to prevent half his crew from being pressed.

After the passage to Gibraltar, the Vigorous entered the harbor there and saluted the governor's flag. An official of the Victualing Board came aboard ship and insisted on inspecting the remaining beer. The issue beer had been mostly expended and the remainder was sour. It was not even good vinegar. Phillips had intended on issuing rum after finishing the beer, but the official insisted on sending out a lighter laden with casks of poor quality red wine. The sailors were to be issued a pint a day.

He learned in port that the tales of insurrection in some French areas, especially around Lyons, Marseille and Toulon were widespread. Hood was thought to be off the French port and important naval base of Toulon. While in port, Burns came to him with an evilly smelling piece of salt beef, right out of the cask. "Sir, the men have been complaining about their meat lately. The cook tells me it started with the last cask opened. I judge it unsuitable for consumption. At my order, he opened a new cask. That was just as bad."

Phillips took the meat and held it to his nose. He was forced to pull the putrid meat away and toss it over the side. There was no way he would eat this himself. "What do we do about this, Mister Burns?"

"Sir, we will need to hold a court of inquiry, consisting of an officer, the surgeon and a respected member of the crew. If the court condemns the beef we can turn it in to the dockyard, but there will likely be a delay when we do it."

"The bad beef appears to be very old stock, but is in new barrels. I suspect some contractor took already condemned beef and put it into new barrels, pocketing the money he would have had to pay for good beef."

"Our orders call for us to expedite, Mister Burns. What if we left immediately and held our court at sea. Any condemned meat we can dispose of over board. We will just keep opening casks until we find some good beef."

"Sir, the Victualing Board requires we return the condemned food. If we do not, they are apt to charge you for it."

"How is the pork?" The ship held supplies of both salted pork and beef, to be consumed on alternating days, with cheese replacing the meat two days every week.

Burns reported the pork was fine.

The board had finished its deliberations on the decayed meat a half hour later and the ship received permission to depart moments later. Once away from the land, the two foul casks were emptied over the side, the empty containers scrubbed thoroughly with vinegar. Phillips ordered pork and cheese be substituted for the beef, until the matter could be rectified.

As they neared the French coast, they spoke a Spanish brig who reported that Admiral Langara of the Spanish Navy with Admiral Hood had entered the port of Toulon and had taken possession of the port.

Entering the inner harbor, Vigorous made her number and saluted Admiral Hood's flag. The salute was acknowledged by both Hood's flagship Victory, as well as a big Spanish three decker. Vigorous' number appeared in the flag's signal hoist, requiring her captain to come to the flag.

Phillips, already in his best, clambered into his boat and was rowed with all haste to the flagship, with the dispatches held firmly under his arm.

Immediately after doffing his hat to Hood, he held out the paperwork, but Hood distractedly passed them off to his flag lieutenant. "I'll look at them later. I think I already know their contents. What are your orders?"

"My Lord, I was to locate you and deliver my dispatches. I am also to deliver dispatches to Ambassador Hamilton at the Court of King Ferdinand in Naples. Following that, I am to report to you for duty."

"Very well, Captain Phillips. That falls in with my needs. I too have a pouch for the Ambassador, which I hope you will deliver. If you will make your voyage to Naples and back, I am sure we will have work for you upon your return."

"My Lord, we have a problem with our provisions. Some of the salt beef we took on in Portsmouth is spoiled. My men are living off the salt pork and cheese that are still good."

"Hmm, can you make Naples with what you have on board?"

"Yes, My Lord."

"Very well, do that. Flags will give you an order to indent on the embassy in Naples to obtain beef there. We have plenty of French beef in warehouses here, but it would take forever to locate it and get it issued. The quality may not be what the men are accustomed to, either. I need you at sea now. You may resupply in Naples."

"By the way, we have a levy on all our warships. We need men temporarily to man the defenses of the port and its environs. You will supply the provost officer that boards your ship with twenty men. They will be returned when we get our expected reinforcements."

The Vigorous left harbor on the evening breeze and set course for Naples. Having aboard a full complement, Vigorous did not suffer from the levy nearly as much as some of the ships, but there were long faces as men left the ship, not knowing when or if they would see their mates again.

Putting out to sea, Mister Avery confessed he did not have good charts for the port of Naples, or the region around it. The ones he had were old copies of older Venetian charts and he didn't know how much he could trust them. On the way to their destination, they ran down a gun brig on a course for Algiers.

The crew of Vigorous hoped for a prize, but the brig displayed her number and the current recognition signal. She was on her way to North Africa to buy cattle for the fleet. Lieutenant Wayne, the captain of the Wolverine, assured Phillips he did have the necessary charts and his master was welcome to copy them. He reported that a pair of galleys had chased them for nearly a day, but they had slipped away after dark.

Vigorous made her way into Naples harbor the next afternoon and fired off the salute. He delivered his pouch directly to the embassy. Ambassador Hammond himself met just as soon as he was announced and took the pouch, excusing himself while he read the contents.

He paid the most attention to Lord Hood's missive. The dispatch from the Admiralty was glanced at and put down.

"I wish Admiral Hood had sent a representative with you. He wishes King Ferdinand to supply troops and seamen to the forces occupying Toulon. In addition to the many soldiers he requires to defend the port, he needs seamen to help man the captured ships The King has some concerns and would like to speak with a knowledgeable military person about the prospects of victory or failure. Could you reassure his Majesty?"

"Your Honor, I was in Toulon harbor for only a day before I came here and never landed on shore. I suspect you know more of the situation than I do."

"Hmm, there is that, Captain Phillips. Perhaps it would be best if you stealthily sailed off into the sunset.

"Your Honor, we do have somewhat of a problem aboard ship. Some of our salt beef stores have proved rotten. Admiral Hood thought we might resupply here."

"Captain Phillips, normally that would not be a problem. King Ferdinand takes pleasure in helping ships of the Royal Navy, often personally. However, in this case it might be better if you did not meet. I think it would be best if you crossed over to Algiers and bought live cattle right on the quay."

"How will I pay for them, sir, a letter of credit?"

"Captain, you will find the Bey of Algiers requires either gold or silver for any purchases made there. My funds are not unlimited, but I can furnish you with enough to purchase a few bullocks, enough meat to get you back to Toulon."

The crew was restive upon leaving Naples. They had all seen the herd of ration bullocks on the quay and after a steady diet of salt pork and cheese they wanted beef, but the particular type of pursefurnished blackstrap wine was especially disliked. Lieutenant Burns advised he thought delegations from the crew could be expected to make their complaints any day now."

Phillips called his clerk to him and began dictating some routine notes he wanted to enter later into the log. As the pair wandered casually to the helm, he dictated to his clerk the order from Hamilton to slope over to Algiers to buy live beef.

There, now the clerk knew their destination and the plan to obtain fresh beef and at least one of the helmsmen had overheard, also. He could expect this news to circulate around the ship by the end of the watch.

CHAPTER FOURTEEN

Pirate

The next morning, well out of sight of land, the mood on the ship was much better. As they proceeded on course, the lookout reported a sail, hull down. As Vigorous approached, Burns came up to him and said, "Sir, the sail appears to be a local trading brig. She is flying no flag and I think there is a galley on her lee. I think the brig has been taken by a pirate.

When the pirate crew realized they had been spotted, they left the prize, tumbled into the galley and set their big lateen sail. At first the pirate angled on the larboard tack toward the North African shore. The frigate, with a following wind, was booming right along and started to slowly overhaul the pirate. Phillips thought he might be able to reach the galley with a few of his forward eighteens. He ordered the ship cleared for action, then, with good men on the starboard guns, told the gun captains on the two forward eighteens to each try a ranging shot.

The most forward gun on each beam was a thirty six pounder carronade. These guns were enormously powerful but their effective range was not great. The next gun astern would be an eighteen pounder long gun. These guns were also powerful weapons but fired a ball half the weight of the carronades, but had greater range. Since these guns could not fire dead ahead, it would be necessary to veer the ship to fire upon the enemy.

The first ball hit the galley's wake a cable to the rear. The next gun, fired when the ship pitched up on a wave, had seemingly grazed the stern of the target. Burns exulted, "Captain, I think we got her rudder."

The galley immediately dropped her lateen and deployed her oars. She came right around to port, using her oars to steer. This caused the galley to slow momentarily as she came to the new course and allowed Vigorous to close the pirate a bit more.

She was going to end up right in the teeth of the wind, an ideal place for a galley to be, since the frigate could not pursue her effectively into the wind. To get there though, the galley had to first pass right by the frigate's bow. Since, like most galleys, she only had a pair of guns in her bows, the Vigorous was in no danger of being raked, but Phillips had an opportunity.

Turning to port also, he followed the galley right around and momentarily found his ship beam to beam with the pirate. Approaching the 'sweet spot', he told Burns, "Fire the starboard guns as they bear."

The mids serving as messengers ran for their respective destinations and gave the order. As the frigate came alongside, her guns started going off, forward ones first. Phillips saw the big iron ball from his forward carronade hit the bow of the pirate low down, smashing a large hole between 'wind and water'. There was other damage to the hull also, so Phillips called, "load, but do not fire."

The oars stopped as the first shots hit the galley and the craft suddenly slowed. The starboard oars got one more stroke than the port oars though, and the galley suddenly turned toward Vigorous. Her port bow gun fired a shot right at Vigorous' bow. The ball hit right forward, causing damage in a very inconvenient spot. The carpenter got to work with his crew, while Phillips told his gunners to fire at the galley's guns, reloading with grape.

The enemy's guns were soon silenced, permanently it developed, when the vessel started going down by the bows and the guns eventually just slid out and went their separate way.

The galley was awash now, with crew scrambling to stay above water. The oarsmen, it seemed, were chained to their benches and unable to escape. Moreover, some of the sailing crew of the pirate, having no other weapons, began popping off muskets. Phillips sailed his ship out of musket range of the stalled pirate and came to the wind.

He sent one of the midshipman messengers to his cabin to get the Fitzhugh rifle and the cartridge box. When the weapon arrived, he extracted a cartridge from the box, tearing the paper tail off at the rear.

Carefully, he poured a pinch of powder in the pan, closed the frizzen and dumped the rest of the powder down the muzzle; he removed the twin projectiles from the remains of the cartridge and placed the projectile assembly down into the muzzle, ramming it home with the ramrod.

Glancing over at the flooding galley, he saw one man preparing to fire a musket. Another was reloading his own weapon. Judging the distance, he felt it was roughly one hundred fifty yards. He had three rear sights on the weapon, one, two and three hundred yard settings. He raised the center sight to the vertical position and aimed at the musket man.

He was swaying too much from the motion of the ship, so went over to the mizzen and leaned against it. Aiming the rifle again, he realized the whole crew was watching. His target, seeing he was going to be fired on, hurriedly snapped off his shot. The ball disappeared, coming nowhere close.

With the sights lined up on the target, he began squeezing the trigger. At the last moment he realized the weapon would strike a little high, so aimed at the red sash the man had about his middle. Almost simultaneously with the distracting flash from the weapon's pan, he felt the silver butt plate slam into his shoulder.

The breeze immediately blew the smoke away and he saw the figure crumbling to the deck. The entire crew cheered. By now the other musket man had finished reloading and fired. This ball nicked the starboard rail. As Phillips reloaded, the new target frantically began the reload drill. Phillips was squeezing the trigger when the man threw his musket over the side.

He almost sent his shot into the blue, then remembered the drowning oarsmen chained to their benches. He sent the load right into the man's chest.

The galley was in bad shape. Its bow had been smashed in and the hull was awash. The vessels had drifted together by now, with no further resistance by the pirate crew. Seamen and Marines were swarming over the wreck.

The ship's armorer was attempting to break the chains on the slaves with his hammer and cold chisel. Slaves were alternately screaming in terror and laughing as they realized they were free of the pirates.

One of the pirate officers, a short, fat man with a magnificent set of whiskers on his face protested when a Marine tried to take his sword. In exasperation, the pirate pulled the scimitar free of his sash and attempted to slash the Marine across the face. The leatherneck parried the blow with his bayoneted musket, drew the musket back and smashed the butt plate into the man's face. As the fool sank to the deck, the Marine pinned the screaming brigand to the gangway with the bayonet.

Phillips, by this time on board the galley's deck with his Captain of Marines commented, "Captain Jones, I surely wouldn't want to go up against your men when their blood was up."

A slave, trapped in his chains at their feet, with his face barely above water spoke, "Sir, that fat bloke your Marine just run through has the keys to these chains."

A word to the Marine sergeant soon had men searching the dead pirate's bloody body. One came up with the ring, heavy with keys. "Your Honor, if you'd stick that big iron key in this lock here, some of us might get out before this scow goes down.", the now spluttering prisoner spoke.

The key was turned in the lock and the man was free. He accepted the keys with a nod of thanks and began freeing the others. Barring those who had been killed during the cannonade, the drowning men were all saved. There would be much work for the surgeon and his mates among both the freed slaves and the wounded now aboard the Vigorous.

After Phillips went back on board the frigate again, the carpenter reported. "Sir, the shot that pirate gave us right up in the bow, did a lot of damage. I've got a sail fothered over the hull and extra hammocks plugging the hole, but we're still taking on water."

Phillips saw his officers, without bothering him, had got the pumps going and water was now gushing from the scuppers.

He could see they were going to be in serious trouble if they could not get the leak stopped. It appeared more water was entering the ship, than was leaving.

Taking stock, Phillips found he had rescued two dozen former galley slaves, with better than half without serious wounds. There were also ten pirates aboard, under Marine guard. Again, about half were free of disabling injuries. He spoke to the Marine's officer and asked him to put the healthy prisoners to work pumping ship.

While discussing solutions to their problem with his sailing master and Lieutenant Burns, a rescued prisoner approached. He informed Captain Phillips he knew of a nearby island where the leak could be repaired.

"Well, please enlighten us, sir", Phillips asked. The men explained there was an island just to the southeast a few leagues that had a good bay with a sheltered beach on the eastern side. "The pirates pull their galleys up on the beach when they have repairs to make." He explained.

"What about people?" asked Burns?

"Jus' a few shepherds and the like and nobody pays 'em any mind."

Phillips asked, "Just how familiar are you with this island, sir?"

"Lord Captain, I ain't no sir. I'm just plain Bill Jenkins. I been chained to these galleys ten year now. I've been to that island upwards of a dozen times."

"What about warships, Mister Jenkins. Do any call there?"

"Never seen none, captain. All the Moor's warships belong to the Bey and he don't let 'em out too much. Liable to go pirating on their own account."

"Have you ever served aboard a King's ship, Jenkins?"

"Yessir, I was a gunner's mate aboard the old Raccoon, on the America station during the last war. Happened I signed on a collier when the brig paid off and a pirate came up the Channel first voyage and took us. I been pulling on oars ever since."

"Jenkins, speaking as a former gunner's mate, do you think it would be practical to land some guns and make a battery to protect us while we work on the ship?"

"Yes sir, no problem at all.

"Well Jenkins, I'm not going to press you after your ordeal. But, if you'd like to volunteer, I'd rate you gunner's mate."

"I'd be pleased to make my mark on the ship's book Yer Honor.

The master went through his meager supply of Mediterranean charts, but found nothing in the area indicated by Jenkins. The ship's officers questioned other members of the galley's crew, both former slaves and the Muslim masters. While none of the officers spoke any variety of Arabic, most of the freed Christians did spoke some dialect, or at least the lingua franca of those parts and questioned their old masters. These worthies were indignant to be questioned by their former slaves and uniformly refused to answer any questions.

The former pirates were put to work pumping ship, with former slaves armed with bosun's 'starters' standing by to 'encourage' them to greater effort. The ship was put to the wind and lookouts ordered to look for any sign of land. It soon became apparent it would be necessary to reduce the influx of water.

Another sail was prepared and fothered over the area of the hull that had been penetrated. The crew began to remove the forward guns from their carriages and placed them on mats, which were dragged to the stern. When 'Land Ho' sounded from the main mast head, they had made a good start in lifting the bows.

Jenkins repeated the beach was on the eastern side of the island. It was of volcanic origin and the cliffs were high and jagged. When they found the beach, it was in an indentation in the cliff. The beach had apparently formed ages ago when a portion of the cliff collapsed and the beach was formed from the rubble. Jenkins said there were only a few people left on the island, since the pirates enslaved any of the locals they could locate without too much trouble.

A bit of the beach, flat and surrounded with earthen dikes, was filled with water. Jenkins said these were salt pans. The locals used them to evaporate seawater to produce salt, which they used themselves and sold to itinerant coastal traders.

As the ship approached the beach, Phillips was anxious to get as much weight off the bows as possible. Empty casks were roused out of the hold and used to make anchor buoys. Bending on lines, they were fastened to the bitter end of the anchor cables and the anchors, cable and all, went overboard.

The master and two lieutenants went out in ship's boats and surveyed the bottom close to shore, finding no gross irregularities. With just a scrap of the fore topmast staysail showing, the ship crept closer to the beach until she touched. Now it was necessary to weigh down the after parts of the

Vigorous. It was thought that sinking the stern, might bring up the bow a bit.

The bow now touching bottom, was a bit higher than it had been earlier and the gash in the bow was now slightly above water. Now the constant pumping was making an impression. The bows were rising a fraction more. Boat anchors were wedged in rocky crevices on shore. Using the capstan, it was possible to pull the ship shoreward a few more feet, raising the bow a little more, in turn causing some of the flooding water in the bows to flow to the stern.

The hull damage was now mostly above water level and the carpenter and his crew went to work on the damage. Cutting away the damaged wood, he fabricated timber in his stores to fit. While the carpenter was working, Phillips had six guns hoisted over the side and used them to establish a battery on shore, enclosing it with rocks and rubble.

One morning, a pair of Marines on sentry duty ashore spotted a boy clambering down the cliffs. Pretending not to notice, they cut him off when he became alarmed and tried to climb back up. The boy, perhaps fourteen or so spoke no language Phillips was familiar with, but one of the freed galley slaves was able to converse with the lad. Phillips gave the boy a silver sixpence and told the translator to inform the lad he wanted to purchase cattle, sheep, or goats, as well as salt to preserve the meat.

Freeing the boy, Phillips suspected they would never see him again, but that afternoon, two more people came down the goat path. One was an old woman, thin and strong, looking as if she were made of dried rawhide. With her was a man of twenty or so, but also looking very capable.

The translator listened to them and reported they would sell many sheep or goats. Each would cost two of the silver coins the boy had been given. Phillips had few sixpences left but held out one of the golden guineas given him by Ambassador Hamilton to buy beef. The woman was stunned. She knew what gold was, of course, but apparently had never dreamed of possessing any.

His men had roused out all the meat casks from the ship's hold and the surgeon and cook had inspected the contents of each. Only six more beef casks were foul. The rest of the beef was still good. The foul meat was discarded and the casks scrubbed out with seawater and sand.

With these six casks to fill, besides the two already emptied, he told the woman he wanted the casks filled with meat, either sheep or goat. He also wanted the necessary salt. She agreed to sell the needed meat and salt for the guinea plus a Spanish dollar she had seen in Phillip's purse. This made her day.

The man ran up the cliff and soon animals started coming down. More natives descended the cliff face and assisted in butchering and cutting up the meat. There was pandemonium as animals were frantically fleeing in one direction or another.

A few managed to escape up the vertical cliff, but most ended up being stretched out on the beach. Phillips left his butcher's crew to their bloody work and returned to the ship.

The carpenter had the hole patched and now the caulkers were pounding oakum and pitch into the crevices. There were no copper sheets to nail over the new wood, but that could wait 'till they reached a proper shipyard. With the ship as light as she could be, it was necessary to get her at sea, before a gale came up that could destroy her on the beach. When the ship was ready to leave, Phillips asked his interpreter what the natives would like as a gift for their help.

The answer was weapons. It seemed that whenever pirates came ashore, some would climb the cliffs and try to capture women and young children. Formerly, they had possessed a musket to discourage the pirates, but that was now broken.

Phillips ordered the gunner to release a dozen of his surplus muskets and bayonets with ammunition. The woman representative thanked him and assured Phillips the natives could now defend the cliff paths to the summit.

The longboat was sent back to look for the large bower anchor. The cask marking the location was soon found and its line was carried back to the ship and brought in through a stern port. It was pulled in until the large anchor cable on the sea bottom took the strain. Then the line was sent to the capstan where it was pulled in until the cable came off the sea bottom, reached the stern port and entered the ship.

With the huge anchor cable at the capstan, the line was cast off and the cable fastened to the messenger cable with a short length of line called a nipper. The messenger was a closed loop between the capstan and a big block up forward. Men at the capstan put the capstan bars to their chests and heaved.

The anchor cable was fastened to the messenger with more nippers. As the capstan turned, the cable was drawn along. When the end of the cable had been drawn forward, the first nipper was loosed and the cable directed to dive down into the cable tier.

Eventually, all the slack in the anchor cable was taken up and now the strain was now between the capstan and the heavy bower anchor on the bottom. With the men heaving on the capstan bars the cable rose from the water, water squirting from the twisted hemp.

At first, the men strained with seemingly no effect, then a wave a little higher than normal slapped at the stern, which was almost afloat. As the big ship rocked, it also moved back a few inches. Phillips stationed an officer at the stern to watch for waves. When he saw a large one approaching, he called out 'Heave' and again and again the ship slid backward. It took the rest of the day, but finally, the ship was swimming free.

The ship was hauled sternward by brute force until it was up to the anchor. Now, the boats were employed in bringing aboard all the stores that had been landed. When enough weight had been brought aboard to give it some ballast, the ship was moved out to deeper water. The guns were brought aboard finally and the tackle and breeching rigged. With everything brought aboard that had been landed and the newly refilled meat casks stowed, the ship was ready to put to sea.

The rules and customs of the Navy stipulated the crew would dine on beef every Tuesday and Saturday. On Wednesdays, no meat would be issued, but the men were allowed cheese, dried peas, oatmeal and a little butter instead. On other days, pork would be on the menu. Because of the difficulties, with much of the original issue of salt beef being corrupt and discarded, the use of pork issued in lieu had nearly finished that article. With full casks of salted mutton and goat flesh aboard, Phillips arbitrarily decreed that mutton equaled beef, while goat was now pork. The cook was ordered to plan accordingly.

An apprehensive captain entered 'La Petite Rade' of Toulon harbor on 15 December. He was of course, weeks overdue and an encountered British sloop of war gave the news that the occupation of Toulon had failed and the forces were expected to withdraw soon. His signal went unanswered for an hour, when he was finally ordered to report aboard the flag.

Arriving there, he was told Admiral Hood was now onshore and Phillips should proceed to the military headquarters.

Hood appeared harried and sleepless. He remained though, the same courteous officer he had been at their earlier meetings. He ignored the reports Phillips offered and just asked what Phillips had been 'up to'.

CHAPTER FIFTEEN

Toulon

Phillips gave his account of his reception at Naples and Hamilton's regret a more senior and knowledgeable military official had not accompanied him. He reminded Hood of the problem with his stores and the inability of Hammond to re-supply him. The account of the encounter with the pirate galley was given and the recovery of the enslaved Christians. Finally, Phillips recounted the damage inflicted upon the Vigorous and the repairs undertaken.

Hood nodded, then shook his head over the report of the missing copper that Phillips had not been able to replace under his bows. He said, "Have an officer and a party of men report to the shipyard here and remove as much copper and whatever other supplies you may need. I must tell you that we will not be able to hold the defenses here much longer. Everything on shore that cannot be taken must be destroyed before we leave."

"My staff will give you a requisition for anything you ask for, but there will not be time to do any repairs. Take your materials aboard ship and prepare to leave. Already, French civilians are clamoring for refuge aboard ship. You have my permission to load as many of these people as may be possible."

"My Lord, what about the party of men I landed when I first arrived? May I take them with me?"

"Captain, I am afraid these parties have been so mixed with other working parties and defense units, that at this point, it would be impossible to locate them. I give you my word though, that all forces, both military and naval, will be withdrawn before we sail. Seamen especially, will be invaluable to crew such French ships in the harbor that we take with us."

At the dockyard an hour later, all was confusion. A frantic bosun's mate said his civilian crew had all left and were now mobbing the various British offices trying to get passage out. Phillips told the mate that he would offer transportation out of Toulon to such shore workers with their families, who would help move his supplies.

By dusk, an increasing crowd was clamoring at the gates. Phillips selected those people as they appeared to transport the material. Some articles were carried on men's backs, while others were transported on carts or wagons. Wheeled vehicles were available, but not the draft animals. Drag lines were attached to the vehicles and humans, both men and women were put to the lines, the vehicles being dragged down to the docks in a rush.

After the news spread, more people had volunteered than could be accommodated, so he allowed the French workers to board ship after completing just one trip. By this time, nobody was bothering with requisitions or records. Whatever a British officer or petty officer wanted, was just carried off.

With all the supplies aboard that he could foresee needing; he brought his people back to the ship. There he saw Captain Jones had the Marines barricading the gate. Desperate citizens crowded the path begging passage away from the port.

The party had to force their way through the crowd. The launch was stationed off the pier, where desperate townspeople could not pelt them with filth.

The launch crew was told to take the items brought from the warehouses and take them to the ship. On return, Phillips ordered the longboat brought along too. When the boats returned, Mister Burns accompanied then. He reported most of the men drafted from the ship earlier in the summer had found their way back and accommodations were now very cramped, what with the incorporation of the rescued slaves into the frigate's crew.

Phillips had promised passage to hundreds of Toulon citizens, who would surely lose their heads if left behind. Looking around in the gathering dusk, his eyes were drawn to the collection of French naval vessels anchored a few cables length away.

"Mister Burns. I want a ship fit to carry as many people as possible away from here. Investigate that French third rate to port. Take some men there with you to look her over. I want a ship that will float as far as Gibraltar. I'm not concerned about armament. She must be rigged and capable of sailing. We have enough stores on board the Vigorous to give her necessary rations and water if necessary. Take the launch and some men and report back as soon as possible. I'll be on the frigate."

It was dark when the launch hooked on and Burns came through the entry port. His uniform was covered with dirt and filth, but he reported the big liner was capable of swimming. "Her upper guns have been removed, but she still has all her lower deck guns. Twenty eight big 36 pounder guns."

"The ship's been more or less abandoned in the harbor for weeks, ever since her crew left. She still has some stores aboard, but from what I saw, it was mostly of poor quality. Her rigging was intact, but the standing rigging was slack and her sticks are liable to go by the board soon if her stays and shrouds are not looked to. She has a suit of sails, but some are in a sad state. She has some old canvas below deck, but we didn't take the time to look at it."

"She has her water tuns aboard, some of them full. I drew some water from the scuttle butt and it was old and brown, but drinkable if one is thirsty enough. As I see it, her biggest problem is, she leaks. She has been taking on water and nobody has pumped her out. If she doesn't get that water out of her, she's going to sink at her moorings."

"Very well, Mister Burns. Which of our officers would you recommend be appointed prize master? One who is capable of sailing her to Gibraltar, or maybe England?"

Burns responded, "Myself sir. I am most familiar with her. I have been all over her. I can start making her ready to sail immediately, given a crew, of course."

"Mister Burns, you will select a crew immediately. Take fifty men with you to get her ready. I want to start sending Toulon citizens aboard. You may draft any males to do any unskilled work aboard ship that they may do; pumping ship for one. Get some good men in the rigging and set her to rights. I expect the Republican forces to enter the city at any moment. If an emergency arises, slip your cable and take her out to sea. Make sure you get necessary charts from Mister Avery. As far as that goes, select a master's mate to take with you.

Before you leave the ship, notify the second officer that he is now premier and ask him now to see me."

Lieutenant Harkins reported to his captain a moment later. "Mister Harkins, you were told you are now first officer?"

"Yes sir, Lieutenant Burns told me."

"For the nonce, Mr. Mullins may regard himself as temporary, acting third officer. I realize he is much too young and has not passed his Board, but we have no one better."

"He has seen more action than some others and has not embarrassed himself or the ship. Would you please give him the news? I am now going back on shore in the launch. I wish Mullins to join me in the cutter. I will be sending French refugees out to both ships, the Vigorous and the French 74 that Lieutenant Burns is preparing. I had better have a file of Marines with me on shore."

"Explain the problem with Captain Jones. Perhaps he may wish to send some leathernecks to the 74, also. Probably, it would be advisable for one Marine officer to remain on the Vigorous and station the other on the liner. There may soon be over a thousand refugees aboard that ship. Finally, I will be sending refugees here. If the crowding becomes intolerable, send the excess over to the other ship."

The mass of people on shore was almost overwhelming. The Marines there were making a supreme effort to control the mass. Most of the people that had helped move stores from the warehouses, were already aboard ship, but many more were inside the main barricade, but behind a secondary one that had been erected to help control the crowd.

The Marines Phillips brought with him joined their comrades and tried to bring order. Phillips, with some effort, managed to climb up on a cask standing on end, near the barricade. He motioned Mullins to climb up on another close beside. The group that had assisted him deliver the materials from the warehouses had swelled by several times, with their families. He asked Mullins to translate for him.

"Silence please." After a few minutes the shouting and screaming subsided. "Citizens of Toulon, many of you helped me carry supplies for my ship. I promised those people I would help them escape."

The screaming and shouting ensued again. Waiting until it died down, Phillips again spoke and Mullins translated, "Citizens of Toulon, I will try to take away as many of you as I can." Before the noise could erupt again, he held up his hand. "There is some need for haste, for it is likely that Republican forces may enter the city at any time." His voice was emphasized by a crescendo of artillery fire. The gunfire had become ubiquitous for days now, but had greatly increased in recent hours.

"Citizens, I have much to say and little time to say it. I assume those people who keep interrupting me do not wish to board ship, so those people should now leave." Shocked citizens began crying and shouting "Non, Non.", before other members of the crowd began elbowing them."

"Those persons inside the barricade have helped us carry supplies, so they and their families will begin loading now. Any persons wishing to fight or cause trouble will be escorted from the area by my men or shot, whichever seems best. If the crowd is not able to control itself, we will simply leave you all here on the quay."

There was a dead silence as the crowd digested this information. The Marines began escorting civilians into the boats. When the cutter filled, the launch took its place. He asked the midshipman commanding the cutter to take it to the Vigorous and ask the deck officer to send the jolly boat, also. Speaking to the crowd again, Phillips informed them that they would be loading in two large ships. Both would travel to the same destination and families should not be concerned should they be separated.

The jolly boat came from the Vigorous with the return of the cutter. The launch returned from the 74 with a towed launch behind it. The cox'n reported the 74, whose name was discovered to be "Franklin" carried her full allotment of boats. This one had been lowered, but there were at present no extra crewmen who could man the oars. Phillips asked from his perch, "Are there any people present who will row this boat? We have not enough British sailors to do this."

Immediately, a half dozen men moved forward. Two sturdily built women followed. With more or less dexterity the eight lowered themselves into the boat and refugees began following. As the boat moved toward the Franklin, it was immediately obvious that some of the oarsmen were not as skilled as they thought themselves to be. The boat did make its way to the Franklin and returned to the dock at the cost of many crabs. The people there cheered when it started taking on board its next load.

Other boats from the fleet began also ferrying refugees out into other ships and by late morning, the crowd had greatly diminished. A French-crewed fishing boat pulled in and also began loading people. Around the harbor, there were still multitudes of people waiting on shore, but those along the quay near the frigate and the Franklin had melted away. Climbing into the jolly boat, with a few last refugees, Phillips had himself rowed over to the Franklin. No crew members saw him come aboard, because,

Phillips judged, the crew was overwhelmed with all the refugees arriving.

Burns rushed up and apologized for not manning the side for him, but the captain brushed him off. The deck was crammed with humanity, but he could see men in the rigging setting it right. A bundle of canvas was climbing the foremast, obviously intended to be a replacement fore topsail.

Asked about the state of the hull, Burns replied the water in the well had dropped a foot since they started pumping. Passengers had been told the importance of the pumps and were lined up to take the place of exhausted people. Hundreds of women were on the ship with their children and the various men in their families. Many of course were from the higher social classes, many who recoiled at doing hard, physical work, as did some men, but others were of the sturdier sort who put many men to shame at the pumps. The stinking bilge water was pumped on deck, where it ran out the scuppers.

Phillips advised Burns to send people around to query passengers to find if any had any seagoing or military experience before descending into the jolly boat to row back to Vigorous. This ship was as jammed with people as Franklin. Mister Harkins had seen the boat approaching and producing the requisite side boys, welcomed Phillips on board ship with a 'hat off' salute with twittering bosun's pipes.

Asked if they could crowd any more people on board, Harkins shook his head. "I don't know how we are going to manage with the ones we have now. Once we get to sea, most of our passengers are going to be sick. It is going to be a sight, on deck and below."

Phillips informed Harkins he was going to visit the flag. He said he had too much to say to try to signal. The cutter was tied up at the bow, her crew resting on the oars. Dropping back to the entry port, Phillips gingerly climbed down the slippery battens. "One of these days, I am going to slip and break my neck" he thought.

Climbing the side of the big first rate, the HMS Victory, Phillips was met by the curious flag captain, who escorted him to his cabin and offered him his choice of Bordeaux or brandy. Accepting the brandy, he swirled the spirit in the glass, warming the liquid with the warmth of his hand. "What can I do for you, Captain?" asked the flag captain.

"Sir, I took it upon myself to load hundreds of French civilians aboard my frigate. I also used fifty of my men to man a 74 gun liner, the Franklin. I then loaded several thousand civilians aboard her. With limited provisions, I would like to ask permission to set sail for a British port as soon as I may."

"My, Captain Phillips. No one could say you have no initiative. Most captains would not dare assume so much responsibility without asking first."

"Sir, I did not want to bother Admiral Hood, with all the responsibilities he has. The civilians were desperate and I hated to deny them. Besides I believe I recall the admiral advising me to rescue what civilians I could. Would you like me to send them ashore? The flag captain grimaced. "No, Phillips, you have merely anticipated the Admiral's orders. Many ships are already loaded down and will be ordered out soon. Formal, written orders will be issued to captains who have not already done so. Tell me about the Franklin. My staff thought her too low in the water to sail. We had thought to burn her, with the majority of the Toulon fleet."

"Sir, I think she will do. She was low, but that was because she has been abandoned for weeks and needed to be pumped out. The civilian passengers on board are pumping her out in relays. She has already risen a foot, even with all the refugees we have loaded aboard."

"What about weapons, I think she had all her guns removed when she came in the inner harbor. Is that right?"

"Not quite, sir. All her upper deck guns are gone, but she still has all the lower deck weapons. Twenty eight guns, all thirty six pounders."

"Ammunition, Captain Phillips?"

"A problem there, sir. I have perhaps fifty rusty balls aboard. No grape or bar shot. Enough powder in casks to make cartridges for that many shot."

"Yes, I think that should suffice. Have you enough people to man those guns?"

"No sir, I have fifty of my crew aboard her to sail the ship. I have just enough people aboard my frigate to fight her, although they will be thin on the deck."

"Hmm, I do believe I could spare, say thirty men for you. Many of them gunners. . Can you fill out the remainder of the gun crews using refugees?"

"I believe I can at least make some noise at anyone that attempts to bother us."

The flag captain scribbled out a note and gave it to him. "Hand that to the watch officer on deck. He will get you your men. You should put to sea as soon as you can. I would strongly recommend you go through your refugees and find any able bodied male who looks like he could serve on a gun crew. Drill them 'till they drop.

I suspect the enemy is mobilizing all of the naval force they can muster. Should you encounter any French warships of force, you may be able to make a fight of it. Remember, if you were to haul down your flag to the enemy, all of your refugees will have an appointment to the guillotine."

After getting the new men carried over to the Franklin, Phillips was forced to send over the extra hammocks that some of his men had 'forgotten' to turn in to the Impress Service back in Portsmouth.

There were no hammocks aboard the Franklin, so these, plus the ones already issued to the men transferred from Vigorous would serve. For the refugees, of course, there was no bedding of any kind available.

Burns appointed some authoritative appearing refugees into deck petty officers, who had the task of assigning areas of the deck for passengers to sleep. Some were upset about the arrangements, but Mullins assured them that any not satisfied would be rowed back to the shore where they could plead their case with the new Republican authorities."

When all the necessary tasks were finished, both ships, with the permission of the flag, slipped their mooring cables and put to sea.

CHAPTER SIXTEEN

Refugees

Captain John Phillips had sailed in colder waters than the December 1793 waters of the western Mediterranean, but many of his passengers had not. The HMS Vigorous was laden with every human being he could cram aboard, refugees of the evacuation of Toulon. Those people 'tween decks were kept relatively warm by the animal heat generated by so many bodies. Many however, simply were not able to find a space below.

These were accommodated by a space on deck, slightly protected by a wrapping of old canvas furnished by the sail maker, serving as blankets. The quarterdeck was kept clear, this being the domain of the officer of the watch. At the present time, this was Acting Lieutenant Mullins, a young man who had just turned seventeen. A crowd of refugees had collected on the fore deck, all huddled together from the cold.

Slightly separate from these people was Sarah Forsythe. She was an anomaly. Her father had been Lieutenant Forsythe, a Royal Navy officer. Her mother was a French native who had married Forsythe two decades ago. After the father was lost at sea near the end of the American war, Sarah was taken back to France at the age of ten to be near her extended family.

The mother had gone into keeping with an elderly gentleman with some pretensions of nobility. The girl had an idyllic life for a few years until the Terror came along. Abandoning their home, the family became transient, eventually ending up in a town near Toulon. Sarah's mother had the vision of somehow getting to sea and travelling to Britain, where she was still a citizen.

The family's dreams ended when another refugee denounced them as royalists in a vain attempt to receive mercy herself. When the mob came, Sarah had been out scavenging for scraps of food and any potential articles of value behind some shops. She escaped, while her mother and stepfamily were dragged off and she never saw them again.

Another person was right beside Sarah on the deck, Pierre Legrand. This person fancied himself a scion of gentility since his grandfather was the bastard son of a baron, so said the rumor anyway. LeGrand had cultivated the diction and the style of his supposed ancestors. Before the Terror, he had often able to convince a maid or serving girl that he was indeed a member of the upper classes and thus a potential way out of the disaster of that woman's life.

Since the advent of the Terror though, he had been forced to suspend the boasts of his ancestry and try to plan how to keep his head on his shoulders. He had somehow made his way to the deck of a British ship of war. He knew the British had the proper reverence of those of noble birth. With some luck, he might be able to parley the rumors of his ancestry into seeming fact.

In the meantime though, he was cold and the ragged young woman next to him was not doing her part. Every time he tried to share warmth with her, she edged away. Deciding to take matters into his own hands, he reached for her and got a handful of the decayed fabric she wore, which tore away. Eyeing the exposed skin, he decided he had a better idea of warming himself. As she whimpered and yelped, he rolled over on top of her. People trying to sleep around them ignored the pair. Sometimes, it was often not wise to notice too many events.

Forsythe wriggled and fought as the man above her tried to accomplish his mission. He would have too, had not Acting Lieutenant Mullins on the quarterdeck seen the struggle.

Normally, lieutenants, when armed, carried a sword. In the circumstances, Captain Phillips had ordered all officers and petty officers to carry arms while on duty. Mullin though, until yesterday, had been a midshipman, armed with a short bladed dirk. He had not had the opportunity since to arm himself with a proper weapon, but was prepared to do his duty with what he had.

Hurrying over to the struggling couple, he considered his options. Realizing the man attempting rape was twice his size, the youth drew the dirk and stabbed down into a heaving buttock.

Legrand jumped to his feet with a roar, but a full grown Marine who had followed Mullins from the quarterdeck, offered to pin the fellow to the foremast with his bayonet. The seamen on watch were there now with line to bind the man up in a cocoon.

When Mister Harkins came to interview the prisoner, Legrand immediately went into his standard spiel, explaining he was of the French nobility and they had different standards than the peasantry.

Captain Phillips was now at the scene and listened to the man without comment. While Harkins ordered the man chained in the orlop, the captain pondered what to do with the terrified woman. He had abandoned his own cabin and sleeping quarters to some refugee women and slung a hammock in the tiny nook where his clerk and servant had slept. These men being relegated to a single hammock jammed into the mess deck which they shared, watch and watch.

The offender, now in custody and unable to cause further trouble, he looked to the woman. She was sobbing uncontrollable and shivering in the cold. Her hands were blistered and bloody. The bosun said in an aside the woman had spent hours pumping ship. Ever since the repair after the battle with the pirates, it was necessary to pump at least an hour of every watch and the refugees now did most of that labor.

An inspiration came to him. His own food pantry was available and while now well stocked, was still capable of stowing a person of slight stature. He told his two youngest midshipmen, boys of twelve and thirteen, to take her there and to rearrange such stores as to allow the slinging of a hammock.

He ordered them to take the woman into his cabin, already occupied by women refugees and show her the quarter gallery; a private privy, normally used only by the captain and his guests, now serving only the women guests. While giving the orders in front of the woman, he never dreamed she could understand his English.

She had stopped sobbing and as the midshipmen started to lead her off, she spoke in upper class English, with a delightful hint of French accent. "Captain, I am dreadfully sorry to have been such a bother. I am very grateful for your compassion and courtesy."

Next morning, while discussing plans for the day with the first lieutenant, the bosun came before him on the quarterdeck, asking whether a cat o' nine tails (a whip used to punish defaulters) would be needed for the prisoner. A fresh punishment device was made up for every miscreant being admonished and it took a fair bit of time to make a new one. Mister Harkins also wondered just how much deck space he might need to clear.

"Mister Harkins, much as I would like to have the prisoner tied up to a grating and given a hundred lashes, I think that is not in the cards. Since he has not been entered on the books, he is not subject to the articles of war. I think we have a choice. We can take him to port in irons and turn him over to a magistrate, to be charged with assault and attempted rape, or perhaps we could simply hand him over to a French fishing boat. Perhaps Mister Mullins could explain to them he is of noble birth and will expect to be treated accordingly."

"But sir, won't the Frogs chop off his head?"

"Well. There is that, Mister Harkins. But I am sure they will do it with the proper ceremony."

The sometimes mentally slow Boatswain, suddenly saw the light and grinned. He said, "My men will keep a good lookout for fishing boats, sir." After all, the magistrate would merely charge the man with attempted rape, ensuring the hangman's noose. On the French shore, he would be undoubtedly be sent to the guillotine as a suspected royalist. In the meantime, Legrand was dragged below, where he was shackled into leg irons bolted to the orlop deck. It would be better for all, this way.

The frigate and liner made their way toward Gibraltar. The canvas aboard Franklin was in very poor condition and had to be husbanded wisely. The Franklin's main masthead was higher than Vigorous', so she was the first to signal "Sail off my starboard bow." Mullins was sent up with a telescope and he soon reported a ship rigged sail ahead, hull down.

A few minutes later, he reported a second. Phillips ordered some kegs of British gunpowder lowered into the launch, along with some 36 pound ball they used for their carronades. When the mid came sliding down a stay to the deck, he sent him into the boat to deliver the ammunition to Burns in Franklin. Before Mullins dropped into the boat, he handed him a note to be delivered to Burns.

In the event of combat, he listed some signals for various maneuvers that might be attempted. He advised Burns to charge all his guns with powder, but to delay loading shot until it was determined what side of the ship would fire. The Franklin had very few balls for the big thirty sixes, so they had to be used wisely.

As the ships approached, it soon became evident the oncoming ships were French and one was a big forty gun frigate, the other a smaller twenty eight. They approached in line astern, the big fellow leading. As they approached, Phillips was concerned about Franklin.

That ship did not have the ammunition or the gun crews to defeat either enemy ship in a drawn out engagement. Her only hope was to overawe the enemy. If the French could be made to believe Franklin was a fully armed battleship, both would likely flee.

He imagined the enemy had recognized the Franklin and perhaps suspected she had been partially or fully disarmed to carry passengers. And what of those passengers? Many of those aboard the 74 were serving as gun crew or at unskilled seaman jobs. Phillips had known his share of British warships that were as badly manned when leaving port.

Gun captains were cautioned to fire only as each gun bore on their target. The French were not shy; they were approaching on the windward side at long pistol shot. At that range, a steady crew should be able to make every shot count.

As the leading ships approached, Phillips saw Lieutenant Granger, his former third, now serving as second officer standing just clear of the bow gun.

When Granger's arm dropped, the gun fired. This was one of the thirty six pound carronades and it made its mark on the forty gun frigate. Then the eighteen pounders started going off, before the French ship fired its broadside.

When it did, twenty guns of its guns fired together. A dozen of them were eighteen pounder weapons. The rest of the guns were the of the French eight pounder caliber. Many of its guns were not bearing on Vigorous, so those were wasted. Every one of the Vigorous' shots hit and by the time the after carronade did its job, some of the forward guns were firing again.

When the French ship passed them, heading toward the Franklin, she was almost a wreck. The mizzen chains had been ruined and the shrouds were loose. The mizzen was swaying. The name on her counter showed her to be the Imperieuse. Phillips saw men called from the guns of the enemy ship to make repairs. It looked like four of its eighteen pounder guns had been dismounted. Perhaps it could not harm Franklin too badly. As the after guns of Vigorous no longer bore on the big French frigate, her forward guns were now bearing on the next ship.

Again the big carronade smashed a ball into the smaller frigate. She was too small and her scantlings too light to see such punishment and it soon showed. The other guns did incredible damage on the frigate. As before, this ship waited before she was almost completely abreast of Vigorous before she fired her broadside. Evidently the French captains did not trust their crews in independent fire.

While he was looking for damage aboard his ship and his opponent, he heard an almighty crash from the Franklin. All her big guns had gone off and savaged the already damaged Imperieuse before she could fire a shot herself. The mainmast started leaning, then came down. The mizzen soon followed, leaving that big ship with only her foremast standing.

The smaller frigate trading blows with Vigorous, due to face that broadside herself in a few minutes, apparently decided it could not take such punishment and bore away to port to try to escape out to open sea. Unfortunately for her, this left her in position to be raked from her quarter, a position from which she could not effectively reply and the real damage started.

This ship proved to be the twenty eight gun Nymphe, a twelve pounder ship. Most of Vigorous' guns had already fired, but the last few eighteens near the stern were still loaded, as was the after carronade. By the time the balls of these guns finished smashing through the ship, the forward guns were loaded and beginning to fire. Her flag came down immediately. Phillips looked to the forty gun frigate. With only one mast standing, many of her guns were masked with fallen canvas and she had lost too many of her crew. When the reloaded thirty six pound long guns of the Franklin came out through the ports, the Imperieuse hauled down her flag.

The Vigorous had received her share of enemy shot and many people were down, both crew and refugees. There was a crescendo of screams as many civilians, as well as hardened crewmen, faced the knife and saw of the surgeon. More from cowardice, than any other reason, Phillips had his barge brought up from where it had been towing astern and was pulled over to the Franklin.

This ship was remarkably untouched. She had received some twelve pounder balls from Nymphe as she tried to bear away, but they were from relatively long range and the thick scantlings kept most from injuring passengers and crew.

He discovered one of the refugees, a former Major of Infantry in the French royal service, had been training some male refugees of military age.

They had few arms themselves, so mostly made do with the few muskets aboard the Franklin, as well as improvised weapons made from swabs. They managed the best as they could, sharing the weapons in turn. The major, an English speaker, believed they could stand and fire in volley soon, if only they had muskets.

Phillips gave orders for the retrieval of the refurbished muskets stored aboard the Vigorous and commended the Major on his initiative. He replied it was to his people's own benefit; if they came into the hands of the revolutionaries, they could soon expect to find themselves a head shorter. He had tried to impress on his men that it was better to die with a musket in hand facing the enemy, than to face a jeering mob from the tumbril on its way to the guillotine.

Phillips then collected seamen and Marines and was rowed to the Nymphe, where he discussed matters with the remaining surviving officer, the second lieutenant, who had been an aspirant recently; the French navy's version of a midshipman. The man spoke English well and the overwhelmed officer agreed to all of Phillips demands. He ordered all French crew members to go below deck and remain there until advised otherwise.

All officers would remain in the wardroom. All small arms except the officer's personal weapons were to be tossed up on deck. Any man, officer or crewman, offering resistance would be controlled by whatever means were necessary. Phillips left his Marine corporal and six men, as well as a dozen seamen on the Nymphe's deck, while he took his boats to Imperieuse where he went on board.

There was no ceremony at all, merely a glowering captain with a bloody arm glaring at him, as if to say for a sou, he would gladly open fire again. A French aspirant did the honors with translation. The French captain refused to acknowledge any orders, so Phillips ordered his sergeant of Marines to escort the captain to his cabin and post guard. He was authorized to restrain the officer, if necessary.

He spoke to the crew member's close by, using the aspirant as translator, "Sailors of France, you have fought honorably and were defeated by superior force. After we reach safe harbor, you will be offered to your government in exchange for British crewmen held in France. With no delay from your government, you may expect to be sent home shortly."

When an excited crewman began screaming at him, Phillips ordered a party of seamen to take him in custody. A man who had gone through the ship, reported there were irons bolted into the orlop deck. The men took him there, where his cries were at least muffled.

Back at the Vigorous again, he found the arms had been distributed and nearly two hundred men drawn up in ranks on deck. Every man was armed with an old Brown Bess musket and a cartridge box of ammunition.

These men were ferried over to the captured ships. The French major went aboard Imperieuse with 100 men. A former magistrate who had served as a junior officer under Lafayette back in the American War was offered command of another 75 men going aboard the Nymphe. Mister Mullins was given overall command of that ship.

Placing Granger in command, of Imperieuse, he went back to Vigorous to make arrangements for towing the captured ships. Not having enough men or material to repair the damage, he felt towing was the last resort. Should that not work, he would be forced to put the enemy seamen into the boats and fire the ships.

The bosun, placed in charge anticipated no problem, as long as the weather did not kick up. Vigorous, being in better condition, with good canvas towed Imperieuse, while Franklin towed Nymphe. The sole sail maker's mate sent to Franklin rifled through Imperieuse' stores of canvas. His intents were to reinforce some of his own mildew damaged sails with better material.

He was able to convince some of Nymphe's sail maker's crew to volunteer to assist; assuring them if they failed to make Gibraltar before the next storm hit, they would all be in trouble.

They were in sight of the 'Rock" when the first ship came out to investigate. After mooring, the prisoners were marched away by soldiers, while the refugees were given shelter until it could be determined what to do with them. Since Sarah Forsythe was a British citizen, Phillips kept her on board, when he found he was to convoy the captured ships to Portsmouth.

Phillips had not consciously noticed the young woman since her trouble on the deck of Vigorous and he was astonished at her new appearance. It seemed the women housed in the captain's quarters had at first been jealous, imagining Sarah to be the captain's toy and treated her at first meeting with great reserve.

With her living below them in the very cramped pantry though, it soon was apparent the captain was paying no attention to her and the women relented. It seemed one had been a ladies hair dresser back home, while the other was a dressmaker.

Taking pity on her ragged appearance, they soon cleaned her up and when the Vigorous sailed into Gibraltar, she appeared as a lady of fashion, beautiful and graceful. Her injuries had healed, along with her spirit. When she appeared on deck, the crew was struck with wonder. She was given Phillips' sleeping quarters, while absent the other women, the captain resumed occupancy of his office.

There were no problems with Legrand. A fishing boat crewed by radical revolutionaries had been overhauled earlier on their voyage to Gibraltar and the sullen crew persuaded to return him to France. Mullins had told them he was a noble in disguise and wished to return to take back his barony, by force if necessary.

The boat crew was told in confidence; he was trying to pose as a radical republican to avoid being taken. The fishing boat crew promised he would be returned to the land of his birth without delay.

The ship made port in Portsmouth and Phillips was dined out more than once by envious officers. For a frigate to use her prize to capture two more frigates was most unusual. There was some confusion of the status of Franklin, because of the circumstance of her taking. However, there was no doubt at all of the Imperieuse and Nymphe and it seemed assured government would soon buy those frigates into the navy.

Phillips posted up to London, taking Forsythe with him after finding that some of her father's relatives lived there. He was reluctant to appear suddenly on her relatives' doorstep with a strange young woman in tow. When reporting to the admiralty he left her in the waiting room, with dozens of young officers in attendance on her. After discussing business with the official interviewing him, he asked that official, a man named Jordan, how he should handle matters.

The elderly, long married man came to the mark. He had an also elderly sister, who would gladly assume the position of duenna to the woman, until she was introduced to her family.

With the man protesting, Phillips imposed his purse upon him, to cover any unforeseen expenses.

Told it would be a matter of weeks before repairs could be made to Vigorous, it would be necessary to disperse the crew to other, more readily available ships coming out of ordinary. Skilled seamen were now a valued resource who must not be wasted on a ship unable to sail for perhaps weeks or months.

Phillips decided to take rooms in the city until he found what the Royal Navy had in store for him. With Vigorous to be out of action for weeks or months, his officers would either go into other ships needing officers or be put on half pay while the crew would be sent to the receiving ship.

With trained crew at a premium, he knew it would be but days before all were scattered to the wind, transferred to such ships that might need them. He asked about Mullins, his acting lieutenant. He was told since the man had not taken his Board, it was unlikely he would be made.

If Phillips was concerned, when he was offered his next ship, he was told he could take the man with him and repeat the promotion at the next opportunity. In a few years, Mullins would be old enough to take the Board and possibly obtain his commission.

A messenger had been sent out and a few hours later the official's sister and a male cousin arrived at the establishment where Phillips was lunching with Sarah and young Mullins. She was a delightful dining companion and he was sorry when the carriage pulled up and she left with her new companions.

Taking Mullins with him, he engaged a cabriolet to take them to an inn. Not remembering any others, he told the driver to take him to the 'King's Arms'. He told himself he had been away long enough for the memories of his past presence in Mary Harkin's life to have dissipated. He decided to take Mullins with him, stop off at the bar and order a meal for the two and just see what developed.

After the pair arrived, they went in. The inn was mostly empty and there was plenty of room. Phillips saw a new serving girl was present, so they were able to sit down with no notice. Steak and kidney pie was chalked on the board, so that is what they both ordered, along with a quart of beer each. The food was good and the beer refreshing, compared with what they were both used to on the ship. After their meal, Phillips ordered port and Suffolk cheese to settle their palates.

As they were enjoying their food and drink, they heard an impassioned "John!" Phillips turned and saw an excited Mary running toward him, her arms outstretched. She put them around him and nearly crushed the life from him.

When emotions subsided, he introduced Mullins. "This is Acting Lieutenant Mullins, of my last two ships. We are adrift here for the nonce, waiting for the Admiralty to grace us with a ship. The last time it took ten years. Hopefully it won't be that long this time."

Phillips turned to Mullins and said, "This is Mary Harkins, a very good friend who has given me some very much appreciated help in the past. I would do a lot for this woman."

Looking at Mary, he asked, "I wonder if that old room of mine might still be available?"

"Indeed it is John. If you wish it, there is a garret room available for your young man, if he requires it."

They quickly settled on a price for the rooms and Phillips and Mary escorted Mullins to his quarters.

Phillips explained to Mullins. "I will be out at all hours so it would be best if you had your own room. Feel free to explore." He fished in his pocket for silver. "Here is some spending money for you."

Mullins protested, "The Lords are in session now. My father is probably there and I can ask him for funds."

"I'm sorry Mullins. I forgot about your father. Please feel free to go stay with him. Stop by here, or send a message once in a while. I'll message you when we are called back to sea."

"Sir, I'd rather stay here, if you please. My pater does not really like to have me around. He sent me to sea so I would not always be inconveniencing him. Sir, do you think I should ask him for money to buy a sword? I don't know if I should buy lieutenant's kit, or whether I will likely stay a mid for a long time."

"Mullins, it might be best to save your money for a while. I did think you had a good opportunity when we had the Vigorous. Now that she is likely gone, I am a half pay captain and you are an unemployed mid. It could be years before you have your opportunity again."

Leaving the boy, Phillips went to his well-remembered old room. Mary was waiting. Uneasy, he asked about her husband. "Ben? Oh, he's dead. He was sitting up in bed one day and just put his hand on his chest and groaned and his head fell down. I sent the pot boy to the apothecary down the way, but when he arrived, he said Ben was dead. Ben's brother went to America just before. It seemed he was in debt and was afraid of being sent to debtor's prison.

The episode of the year before was forgotten and John Phillips related some of his adventures since then. He told her of the funds he had acquired from the capture of enemy ships and the several thousand guineas that he was awaiting. Mary went to her door and called her maid-of-all-work and told her she would be in this room for a while and ordered the bar man to handle the taproom for the remainder of the evening.

John remembered about the rumors of the past and asked Mary if she had any concerns.

"Of what? My husband is dead. I own outright half of this inn. My brother in law owns the other half, but he is afraid of going into debtor's prison and has fled to America. I am paying a few shillings a week to his creditors, just to keep them from coming after this property. I don't think anyone can touch me.

CHAPTER SEVENTEEN

HMS Courageous

Spring in the New Year was coming late and John Phillips was becoming mired in stress. A few months before, the solicitor representing the person owed money by Mary's former brother in law came to the inn and offered to settle the matter for a sum of five hundred pounds.

Apparently, the plan was to seize Amos Harkins' share of the business through the court and sell it to her for that sum. Phillips protested the entire business was not worth that much. Mary had been paying a few shillings a month to keep the wolves from the door. This apparently was not enough for the parties concerned though and Mary had begun to hint that perhaps he could loan her the money. Every day the tears seemed to start flowing earlier and Phillips would start thinking of where he could go to get away from them.

After finding some of his old, fish selling clothing, he even began accompanying his former helper on his rounds, just for an excuse to get away. The horse was glad to see him, anyway. The suggestions now started to come; perhaps this would be a good time for the two to be married.

After all, she did have a dowry of half a business. What did he think of a June wedding?"

At that time, one of his prizes was adjudicated and he was flush with funds. Also, a letter had arrived from Admiralty requesting his 'presence for consultations'. Phillips had no idea of what that entailed, but he could think of nothing he had done that was too criminal. Another problem looming on the horizon was Mister Mullins. Apparently the seventeen year old had become enamored of a fifteen year old maid in the inn.

John had met the boys' father at his club recently. Actually, he was not a bad sort, just not the man to be a father. With him was his friend, the good Commander the Lord James George Mortimer, Earl of Brumley.

Brumley seemed not to recognize him, but offered the respect Phillips was owed due to his captaincy. Mullin's parent said he appreciated the training the boy was being given and wondered when he might be going to sea again. Brumley seemed not to want to offer any input here, so Phillips said he himself was on half pay and could not do anything for the boy until he had a ship.

He did remind the father Mullins had been aboard his last two ships and had proved to be a dependable officer. He related how he had promoted the boy to an acting lieutenancy, but that fell through with the paying off of the ship,

"How would we go about getting the boy made a regular lieutenant, anyway?" asked the father.

"There are ways to get around this, but legally, the boy should be twenty, with six years sea time under his belt, before he can take his board. There have been exceptions, but these take a lot of 'interest'. I might mention the boy has only four years sea time."

"Hmm, perhaps no one has noticed he spent four years on the books of HMS Sandwich when he was between the ages of eight and twelve."

"Sir, I had understood he was attending school in Paris during those years."

"Well, of course he was not actually at sea then, but he was on the books and I imagine they could be produced."

"My Lord, I am but a simple sailor, promoted to my present rank through good luck. If I presumed to meddle in matters above my station, I would probably regret it. However, I will be pleased to do what I can for the boy as soon as I am able. The moment I get a ship, you will see him on my quarterdeck."

Before Phillips left the club, Mullins parent slipped something heavy into his pocket. Once outside, he examined the article. It proved to be a rouleaux of guineas. He gathered he was expected to use the money to care for the boy until something came along. That was no problem. He enjoyed having the young man around. As he saw it, the first thing he needed to do was get the boy away from the young maid. The boy's father would not be amused if the girl found herself with a bun in the oven.

At the inn, he asked the maid to collect Mullins and tell him to report at once. The girl covered he mouth as she tittered, then ran off. Mary caught him as he was stuffing clothing into his sea chest. "Oh, don't just jam your things in there like that, John. I would have done it for you, if I had known. Are you going away?"

He showed her the letter from Admiralty. "Who knows what this is about? I don't know what they want. I just want to be ready for all eventualities." At the spur of the moment, his mouth ran away. He said, "Mary, I need pen, ink and paper."

When she produced the items, he realized he could change his mind and scribble an innocuous list of some sort. However, he did as he had meant and penned a note of hand to her in the amount of five hundred guineas. Without words, he handed it to her.

She looked at it for a moment, then held him. "John this means???"

Phillips said, "Just pay the solicitor. Make sure you get a receipt from him and it should indicate there are no further liens on this property. Maybe you should get a solicitor of your own to insure you are protected. As I recall, they asked for five hundred pounds. You have five hundred guineas, giving you some extra funds to engage a solicitor. I suggest you do so."

"John, you aren't leaving for good, are you? Please come back."

Feeling like a scoundrel, Phillips said, "I may have to go back to the Navy for a bit. Don't worry, you'll see me again."

He met Mullins outside the building and the pair caught a cabriolet carriage to the Admiralty building. "Sir, are we going to sea?"

"I don't know, Mullins. Probably not. They want my advice about something. Probably want to know how the proposed Sea Fencibles should be outfitted."

"Well sir, why did we need to pack our sea chests, then?"

"I needed to get out of the inn for a bit. Maybe we'll go up to Scotland for a time. What about you? Are you anxious to get back?"

"I don't know, sir. Molly is a very nice girl. She wants to get married. Says my father can give us money to buy a cottage and we could then live well."

"Mullins, you are seventeen. Best wait a few years until you can stand on your own feet, without needing to run to your father for funds every glass."

At the Admiralty, Phillips took a seat in the crowded waiting room. Mullins was forced to stand in the rear. Another man standing in the rear was Lieutenant Burns, his former first lieutenant. A brief chat with the officer produced the information that Burns had been frequenting this room all winter, in hopes of getting a ship.

After only an hour of exchanging sea stories of half pay status with another captain, Phillips was called. He was ushered to the same office he had entered a few months ago, with the same official behind the desk.

"To business, Captain Phillips.", Mr. Jordan offered.

'We have a ship to offer you. It is the HMS Courageous, a 36 gun frigate, eighteen pounders. Much the same as your last. She is a little larger. Actually, she is still in commission, with her crew still on board. Her present captain is Captain Aikins, the Member for Milton, who has certain responsibilities in the House and desires to retire from the sea. He has had to take much time off in recent years from his naval duties, taking on job captains to handle the ship. Courageous is in port, ostensibly to obtain some carronades, but really to install a new captain."

"With Captain Aikins being absent so much and various job captains coming and going, the ship and crew are reported to be in dismal condition. Admiral Parker has stated he does not want the ship under his command. Perhaps her first lieutenant is to blame, perhaps not. Aikins, from his leadership position in Parliament has managed to protect the premier from his supposed shortcomings, but the problem cannot continue."

"Just who is this officer?"

"Perkins, a nephew of Captain Aikins. He has only been commissioned five years, serving much of that time in the halls of Parliament as a sort of equerry to his uncle. This required Captain Aikins to employ very junior officers so Perkins can remain first lieutenant. Aikins, from his seat in Parliament has great power to influence the posting of these junior officers. A major problem of the Navy is the lack of sea experience among some of these politically appointed young people."

"Sir, in the waiting room, I noticed a former first officer of mine. A man of ten years commissioned service or more."

"Captain, I doubt if Captain Aikins would let us get away with replacing Perkins with your officer as first lieutenant straight off."

"Sir, would you have a ship, possibly needing a lieutenant that would be sailing for foreign shores soon?"

"Well, there is the Ajax '74, escorting a convoy to India next week."

"Sir, suppose we let things go for a bit. I could take command of the Courageous whenever the Navy wishes. A few hours before the Ajax sails, Lieutenant Burns, my old first officer is ordered aboard Courageous to fill a vacancy we arrange. He ranks Perkins out of his job. Perkins can either request in writing that he go down to second officer to gain experience or he could be bundled aboard Ajax at the last minute."

"That could possibly work. Let us hold off for a while until we see how matters work out when you take command. In the meantime, the Miss Sarah Forsythe you steered our way wishes to meet you again before you sail away. My sister is impressed with the girl and wants to employ her as a companion, but her uncle wishes to claim her himself. Do you suppose you could come to dinner at our home tomorrow?"

"Barring any last minutes problems aboard the Courageous, I can see no reason why not."

"Why not go aboard now, get matters straightened out and then tomorrow afternoon, I will have my carriage pick you up on the quay. Have you any questions or comments?"

Collecting Mullins and their sea chests, Phillips debated whether he should signal Courageous to send a boat. He decided it would be easier to just hire a shore boat to take them out. They found a wagon to carry their chests to the quay and engaged a wherry to take them out. The boat was challenged, but when the boatman called out "Courageous", there seemed to be confusion aboard.

A young lieutenant came to the entry port and protested that Captain Aikins was the captain and no other officer who announced himself as "Courageous" was allowed aboard. Phillips had drawn his boat cloak back and was plainly displaying his epaulet on his right shoulder."

Not wanting to get into a long range arguing match, Phillips said, "Very well, Aye, Aye." He was indicating merely that a commissioned officer wished to come aboard, with no mention of him being the captain. Side boys traditional for a visiting captain appeared and the lieutenant stood by the entry port, his hat off in salute.

Phillips, after donning his hat offered his commission. "Lieutenant, would you please read this to the hands?"

"Sir, I cannot do this. Captain Aikins is still in command."

"Lieutenant, will you at least please read the damned thing to yourself."

The officer quickly glanced over the document. "Notice the signature? That is the First Sea Lord of the Admiralty who signed that. Have you ever, sir, seen a man hauled up to the mainyard at the end of a line? That is what they do to mutineers. I am told it is quite painful."

"But sir, I was told ….!"

"Mister, I am rapidly losing my patience. I would strongly suggest you gather some men so I can read myself in, if you will not."

The officer turned to a bosun's mate and ordered, "All hands, gather on the main deck."

CHAPTER EIGHTEEN

Opium

The ceremony had been unduly delayed and Phillips imagined the boatmen were probably annoyed, so he leaned over the side and dropped a few coins into the still waiting boat. He remembered seeing no ship's officers on deck save the young man who had met him at the entry port.

As he wondered, he saw a portly looking Marine captain puff his way to the quarterdeck. His scarlet uniform was spotless and his leather accessories gleamed with polish. He approached and saluted
Phillips smartly.

"Sorry Captain, for my absence on deck when you came aboard. I was not told. My name is Caruthers."

"Captain Caruthers, please look at my orders and satisfy yourself of their authenticity."

A quick glance brought a statement, "They look quite authentic to me, sir."

"Would you look at them more closely? In case you are asked to testify before a court martial, I wish you to be able to state whether or not you believed I am your lawful captain."

The officer slowly read over every word of the orders. "Sir, I recognize the signature of the First Sea Lord. I am satisfied."

"Well then, am I correct in believing this ship is in a state of near mutiny? Are your men under control and will they obey orders?"

"Oh sir, they will obey you and do their duty, as far as that goes. The thing is, I only have a dozen Marines on board. You need to understand, this ship does things differently."

"Caruthers, as I am the captain, everyone will do things my way; that is the Royal Navy way. I want all your men formed up now on the quarterdeck, armed and in uniform."

As the officer puffed his way below, Phillips realized many of the hands brought up to witness the change of command, had drifted below again. Those men still on deck appeared almost lackadaisical.

Turning, he saw Mullins behind him. "Mullins, how are you with signals?"

"Sir, I can remember a lot of them, but I would be better if I had the signal book."

"Do you think you could send the signal, 'Ship not under discipline', Require Marines. Address it to the flag."

"Yes sir, I think so."

"Do it now, please?"

Phillips noticed the officer that had met him at the entry port was looking out over the harbor, ignoring everything behind him. Two Marines came thundering up the ladder from below. One approached, came to quivering attention and saluted. "Sah, Corpril Jackson sir, Party of two. Rest of my men will be here shortly, only some don't have full uniform, Sir."

"Well, get them up here with what they have, so long as they are armed."

Five minutes later, the rest of the Marines were formed up on the quarterdeck, in a motley collection of red uniform and purser issued slop clothing. The clothing they did wear appeared donned helter-skelter. Caruthers appeared before his men, sword in hand."

"Sir", reported Mullins. "Flag answers, "Query?"

"Damn", thought Phillips. "With my problems here, I'm faced with an idiot on the flagship that can't read signals."

"Mullins, are you sure you got that signal correct?"

"Yes sir, there was a book in the signal locker."

"Well, send the damn thing again and keep it flying. Maybe one of the water hoys will read it."

Phillips noticed some telescopes around the harbor focusing on their signal. Suddenly, he saw a launch behind the Ajax being brought up from astern. Red coated Marines began tumbling down into it and seamen were soon bending to their oars. A few moments later, the launch had hooked on to the chains of the frigate and men were pouring aboard.

A red faced ship's captain was facing him, while the Marines he brought with him formed up in front of the new captain. He held out his hand in greeting and said "Billings, from the Ajax. We saw your signal and thought to come calling. I was warned you might have trouble taking command."

Mullins broke in, "Sir, signal from flag. Boat to arrive with Marines and officer."

Phillips was explaining the circumstances to the new captain, but was mystified when he saw the officer who had originally met him at the entry port slowly going down the ladder to the wardroom. When the lieutenant from the flag arrived with another boatload of Marines, it was decided to have both watches of the Courageous crew come on deck for inspection. It was then that the flag signaled, "Send officer".

Billings noticed his confusion. Who to send? He said, "Let us visit your wardroom and see what you have to work with."

Going below, they both noticed a strong pungent smell, almost overpowering. "That's opium", remarked Billings. You are commanding a ship of opium eaters." In the wardroom, a lone officer sat, staring off into space. When they started opening doors, they found other officers and warrants in a stupor.

"Captain Billings, if I could have the loan of a few of your Marines, I'd like to take this officer across to the flag with me. I think he would be the best way to explain to the admiral what we have here.

The intoxicated lieutenant, bound into immobility and lashed to a carrying board was lowered into Ajax's launch and carried to the Flag. The duty watch on deck, seeing the state of the passenger lowered lines to raise the patient on the carrying board. Phillips saluted the quarterdeck and raised his hat to the newly promoted Rear Admiral Elphinstone, whose curiosity would not permit waiting longer to find what was going on.

"Your report, Captain." Elphinstone demanded.

"Sir, earlier this morning, I went aboard HMS Courageous, to assume command. The officer on deck, initially declined to allow me to board. When I did board, I asked him to assemble the crew so I could read my orders. He did not want to allow this. A bosun's mate called 'All hands" and I read myself in to a group of sailors."

"It was soon determined most of the crew was in an advanced state of intoxication. Captain Billing of HMS Ajax, now on board with a detachment of Marines, says the men and officers have been smoking opium.

Many are insensible, but I have brought with me a ship's officer who was found in a dazed condition at the wardroom table." He pointed to the figure lashed to a board at the entry port.

"Call the doctor. Pass the word for the doctor."

That warrant officer examined the patient and smelled his breath. He reported, "This officer is in an advanced condition of opium intoxication."

"So doctor, you are saying this officer is an opium eater?" asked the admiral.

"Certainly he is addicted to the smoke of the substance", said the surgeon. "He must never again use opium, in any form."

When Phillips was rowed back to Courageous, Billings was waiting for him. "What is happening?" He asked.

"Admiral Elphinstone has assembled an ad hoc court martial which will be boarding soon to investigate. He has already personally passed judgment on Lieutenant Grafton, my ship's third officer, based on my testimony and that of Mullins. He is to be dismissed the ship immediately and will likely face a court martial with the other officers. He was at the most, semi-conscious during the proceedings and I doubt he will have much memory of it."

"You seem to have sympathy for him?"

"Not really. We have both known plenty of officers, who have been frequently drunk and incapable from alcohol, men that were tolerated in the wardroom for years."

All crew members were removed from the ship and placed in barracks ashore under guard by Marines. The court stripped all warrant officers of their warrants. The now missing premier was dismissed the service. Shortly after, his body was found bobbing in the harbor.

Apparently, he had stepped through a stern window and drowned. The Corporal of Marines that had answered Phillips first request for assistance was found 'not guilty' and returned to duty, as was the bosun's mate who had called the hands on deck to witness the new captain read his orders.

Many of the seamen were to be replaced man for man without punishment. Every ship in harbor, before sailing, transferred over its quota of people, to be replaced by the incriminated men of the Courageous. It was felt; once the ship was at sea, there would be little opportunity for the damaged men to obtain opium again.

New men were coming aboard in trickles. A pair of young lieutenants, fresh from half pay and the Admiralty waiting room shared one boat. Phillips welcomed them with enthusiasm; at least he would not need to do everything by himself now. One passed him a note sent by Burns. He was going to retrieve his chest and would be aboard shortly.

Seeing a carriage pull up on shore, he looked through his telescope. He expected to see an official of some sort and he was correct. The official he saw was not quite what he expected, though.

Through the glass, he saw Mister Jordan, his sister and Miss Forsythe. What to do. With all the activity, the planned visit to the Jordan home was out of the question. He could not possibly go ashore on personal business with the ship in its present state. Looking forward, he saw the new officers at work, supervising. Mister Haley was up forward inspecting the fore chains and shrouds. Mister Gregor was peering down a hatch, looking at something.

Gregor had removed his blue coat, in all probably the only one he owned and had slop clothes on. Haley however, while he had removed his good coat, still was clad in a worn and tattered older one that was serviceable.

"Mister Haley, Will you kindly attend me?"

Handing the officer his telescope, he said, "Sir, would you examine the party standing by the carriage on the quay, please?" Phillips asked. "The gentleman is Mister Jordan of the Admiralty. One of the others is his sister and the young lady is a friend of mine. Unless I miss my guess, Jordan was instrumental in assigning you and Gregor to the Courageous and rescuing the pair of you from half pay. Would you be so good as to take the cleanest looking boat ashore and invite the party aboard? I was invited to his home this afternoon, but due to events, I find myself unable."

Haley appeared distressed, probably because of the state of his dress and the appearance of the ship, but wanted to impress his new Captain with his activity and said "Aye aye sir."

The barge was rowed to shore with a new boat crew, replacements that had been drafted from several ships. Phillips, in uniform, approached the master's mate of the watch. "Wilkins, that party on shore will be coming to the ship in the barge. Better have a chair ready for the ladies. I don't know about the gentleman. He is from the admiralty but is a civilian. When he comes aboard, whether by chair or through the entry port, have Marines and side boys, as though he were a captain."

Miss Jordan was the only one needing a chair. Forsythe and Mr. Jordan both climbed the battens like veterans, Sarah removing her slippers first. Everyone ignored the unpleasant circumstances of the previous day. Jordan told the women the ship would be leaving at any moment for service across the channel and everyone must make their farewells soon. While the Jordans walked the deck, Sarah and John discussed meeting again. Phillips told her he looked forward to showing her around London, but his time was not his own at the moment.

CHAPTER NINETEEN

Secret Documents

A day later, the ship left the Pool of London, descended the Thames to the sea and was facing the chop of the Channel. All the former officers and warrants had been replaced with all possible speed. The premier, whose body had been discovered in the harbor, was superseded by Mister Burns, Phillip's former first lieutenant on the Vigorous.

Haley and Gregor had taken hold immediately and were now valued members of the crew. All members of the wardroom were newcomers, but rapidly becoming acquainted. The officers were relaxing over the captain's table, after the nerve wrenching task of coming down the Thames to the sea. A couple of 'dead soldiers' were already rolling on the deck.

"But sir", wondered Burns, "How did an entire ship's crew become addicted?"

Phillips explained the recent history of the Courageous, how its former captain was frequently absent for weeks or months, being replaced by job captains. He told how the court martial had discovered that early on, under the aegis of one of the job captains, the frigate had captured a French prize coming back from India laden with opium. This material was taken aboard the frigate and the prize was then burned.

Later, after Captain Aikins resumed command, he had one of the chests removed to his quarters, sending the remainder ashore. Early in his naval career, Aikins had visited China and had experimented with smoking the substance. Decades later, he remembered the peace the opium smoke had given him. Inserting a small bit of opium into a hole poked into the tip of a cigar, the delights of the smoke came back to him.

One of his officers, plainly under a deal of stress had also been furnished some of the drug and instructed how to use it. Soon nearly the entire crew was using the drug. Aikins, now back at his seat in Parliament, decided he no longer wanted to sail and told his premier he would use his influence to gain the man his captaincy.

Once, the Navy had been awed by the man and his political power, but lately, with his increasing confusion, even members of his own party began treating him as a leper. It was beginning to be felt by some people that there was a strong possibility he would not be returned in the next election.

It was a blustery day when Courageous met up with the Channel Fleet off Brest and made her number. Lord Howe's flagship, the huge first rate of 100 guns, Queen Charlotte, displayed the Courageous' number, with the signal, 'Captain, repair on board'. The crew of the frigate, astern of the flag, immediately brought its launch around and the boat's crew tumbled in,

Phillips following more sedately. Aboard the Queen Charlotte, he was escorted into Admiral Howe's quarters. Seated at the dining table, wine and small pastries were brought and Howe initiated the discussion.

"Well Phillips, is your ship going to infect the fleet with talk of mutiny?"

He explained to the admiral how the crew had been plied with opium by their old captain. He assured him the former officers and warrants had been dismissed and a new leavening of petty officers had been supplied.

"How are your hands getting along since their opium was taken away?"

"Sir, most of the heavy users have been replaced by seamen from other ships. A few of them that we still have on board will approach an officer occasionally to beg for the material. All of the opium Captain Aikins brought aboard was landed in London."

"The only such material on board is a little laudanum in the hands of the surgeon. I have forbidden him to dispense any of it without my permission. When a man seems to me to be overly anxious, he is sent to the pumps for a while. My surgeon tells me exercise is a specific for the treatment of opium withdrawal.

"Very well, Captain. I ordered the various ship captains in the fleet to forbid any of your boat crews to approach within earshot. I want no news of this disaster to come aboard my fleet. Orders have been written for you. Your ship will patrol up and down the channel coast, causing as much difficulty for the French as possible. Should you encounter anything remarkable, you will report it at once. I hope you understand that I want no communication between my fleet and your ship. Eventually, the news will filter out from home. By then I hope other news will dilute this. Have you any questions?"

Phillips gave Burns the crux of the orders on the quarterdeck. "We are not to come within earshot of any ship in the channel fleet. Admiral Howe does not want the news of the mutiny to escape. We are ordered to patrol up and down the French coast with the idea to make ourselves obnoxious. I had a similar mission in another ship last year and it proved profitable. Hopefully, it will be so again.'

The big frigate did find plenty of targets. Unfortunately, many were small, coasting type craft that proved adept in escaping the warship. He did capture several small craft caught unaware coming around headlands, but since they were of little value, Phillips burned them. There were long faces among his crew, but he dared not send men away in low value prizes, knowing it might be weeks or months before he might get them returned, if he got them back at all.

He had been wishing he could exercise his gun crews using live fire. The Admiralty did not believe in the promiscuous use of ammunition at sea and there must be a good reason for its expenditure.

One afternoon, they were cruising along the coast, when they found a large town at the head of a good harbor. Wishing to improve the master's charts, he invited that worthy, as well as two of the officers to mount to the three mastheads, to put their ideas of the scene on paper.

The two lieutenants proved not to be inspired artists, but the new master, Mister Ranson was a different matter. His drawing was a masterpiece, meticulously drawn to scale. Going over the paper, Phillips noticed a building on it that seemed to have more detail than the masthead view should have presented.

Ranson admitted to having gone ashore there in the days before the Revolution and staying in the posting inn, for that was what that building was. He had drawn in the pens where the relief teams for the big coaches were kept and the large barn.

Well, anyway, he had found an excuse to expend ammunition. Military targets were always legitimate objects to fire upon. Freshly dug earth showed where the local military artillery unit was installing a new battery.

It was not complete, and did not appear to be functional yet. Pointing it out to the premier, he asked him to casually edge the ship into gun range, being ready to instantly trim the ship to the offshore breeze and retreat if necessary.

On the way in, he instructed Burns to watch over the guns, assigning such midshipmen to gun sections as he saw fit. These boys had newly come aboard and he had no idea of how adept they would be in their profession. While most had a least one commission under their belts, they were also the ones their last captain had decided he could do without.

The master he asked to conn the ship, making sure they did not come to grief in the harbor on an old wreck or uncharted bar.

At long grape range Phillips gave the order to run up their ensign. There seemed to be no notice taken by the scurrying soldiers on the beach, busy with their tasks. It appeared the troops were still excavating positions for the big guns and the magazines. No artillery was present, as of yet.

As he watched, two columns of troops doubletimed toward the emplacement, preceded by a large tri-color flag. Then, a pair of horse drawn guns, four pounders probably, came clattering up to the beach. As the horses were led off and the limbers unhooked, Phillips announced, "Your target is two enemy guns. Fire when your guns bear."

There was a delay, as midshipmen checked the aim of their guns. Burns expostulated with one gun captain over the position of that gun's quoin. Apparently, it had been shoved all the way forward, as it was pulled out a bit while Burns watched.

The officer handed the lanyard to a small 13 year old midshipman. Holding the lad by the shoulders to prevent him getting in the way of the recoil, he whispered in the lad's ear. The boy yanked on the line and the gun exploded in smoke and flame. A jet of flame shot out the muzzle followed by a cloud of smoke.

The other guns in that broadside began to fire, as their gunners got them aligned. After each gun recoiled backward, its crew began with their reload drill. When the breeze rolled the smoke bank away, the results were laid bare to the ship's crew.

There had been eighteen balls sent down range. At least two of the eighteen pound iron balls had impacted the two small guns on the shore. The guns and their carriages were smashed. The only piece standing was a lone limber. The premier went to a four gun section and ordered them to fire on the remaining limber, reloading with grape after the loaded ball was expended. Each gun fired, every shot impacting away from the target, except the last. The final charge hit the limber and it dissolved into its component parts.

The remainder of the guns were now ordered to fire on the military construction crews, who were standing immobilized watching the show. Most of the guns that were still loaded with ball were not all that impressive to watch. But all four of the most recently fired guns were now loaded with grape and the eighteen pound packages of iron plums were awesomely deadly on troops standing in the open. Enemy soldiers were falling over in ranks and files. Soon, there were no more targets left worth firing upon.

Quiet having returned to the shore, Phillips ordered the launch and cutter loaded with armed seamen and Marines sent to the shore. With the ship's guns loaded and pointed at possible trouble spots, the landing party scouted the area, collecting tools and weapons. The gun barrels, from the destroyed battery were man-handled into a shore boat, carried out in the harbor, then sank in place.

The seamen were sent into the town, searching for any military materials they might need to destroy. His servant Hodges, appeared before him, asking to be permitted to go into town to purchase cabin stores.

After some thought, Phillips agreed. "Take Midshipman Mullins with you. He speaks French and may be able to keep you from being cheated. Tell Mullins to take two Marines with you. If you miss the ship, all of you will end up in a French prison."

A messenger from the shore party returned to the ship, reporting that a dozen horses had been found in the pens of the posting inn and had all been turned loose and driven out of town. Phillips thought this might have been overkill, but the horses were now free and not able to be utilized by the French until much effort had been expended capturing them.

At dusk, with no reports of enemy activity, Phillips ordered the saluting cannon fired. This was the signal that all forces were to withdraw to the ship. His glass fixed on the shore, he finally saw Mullins, the marine guards and the servant running for the shore. The longboat edged in to take them aboard and began to row the party back to the ship.

With the advent of dusk, Phillips gave orders to take the ship to sea, then went below to retire. He had just made himself ready for bed, when he heard Mullins outside arguing with the sentry.

Irritably, he called for Mullins to enter. "Sir", said Mullins, "we were just making ready to return, when a carriage drove into town. There were four outriders, armed and in French military uniform. I understood from the inn's staff this was an Army mail vehicle that came through every week this time with military dispatches.

The servant I talked to, did not realize that I was

British and said they would have to remain overnight, because all the post horses had been freed. They would need the overnight hours to feed and rest their own horses. We had to leave suddenly when someone realized we were strangers ourselves and Hodges was a foreigner. I don't think they recognized our Marines' uniforms.

"This carriage, you saw, when will it leave?"

"I understand it normally stops just to change horses. Theirs were pretty well blown and they will have to stay overnight, unless someone brings in some of the animals we turned loose."

"Which way was the carriage travelling, Mister Mullins?"

"East sir, toward Caen."

A word with Burns readied the ship and Ranson took her out. His subconscious woke him in the early hours of the morning watch. He came on deck and asked Lieutenant Haley for their approximate position. Being told where the guess placed them, he checked the chart. On shore, he noted was a small bay that the coast road closed. There was no town or village present, nor did the bay permit a ship with the draft of Courageous approaching close to the shore. A land breeze held the ship away from the land and barring a shift, she was safe for now. After some thought, he ordered Haley to approach as close as practical to the shore and prepare all ship's boats.

At first light, the boats were loaded with armed sailors and Marines. Despite the pleas of Burns, Phillips took command of the landing party and took the boats ashore. While there was a beach of sorts, a ten foot cliff prevented easy access to the road. A sort of goat path up the side of the cliff however, permitted them to climb up and observe a stretch of the coast road. No traffic being in evidence, men were stationed on each side of the road in a blocking position.

There were plenty of trees along the road and axe men were put to work felling some. Trees were laid down on the coast road, angling in the direction from which the carriage was expected. The men struggled with fatigue and boredom until about four bells in the morning watch, when the squealing of an ungreased axle was heard. The noise came from behind and soon, a small cart, drawn by a missmatched pair of cattle, one a bullock, the other a cow. The driver stopped at the obstruction and appeared bewildered. Mullins went over and inspected the vehicle.

"Just farm produce, sir. The man is taking it to market in the village."

Phillips was anxious to get the cart removed before the carriage arrived. He walked over to it. It held a box of over-wintered potatoes, a bag of spring greens, a container of wrapped packages of butter and some wrinkled apples. He told Mullins to tell the driver he wanted to buy the whole load.

The driver wanted to bargain, but time was a commodity they did not have. Phillips drew a pair of golden guineas from his purse and told Mullins the man could have them if he dropped his load and left instantly. Mullins was shocked. "Sir, you could buy his whole farm for that money. I can get it for much less."

"Mullins, I have no time to bargain or argue. Will you obey me or not?"

A quick "Yes sir" got the desired results. The wondering driver, delighted at his good fortune, turned his empty cart around and left. The landing party had hurriedly removed the produce to the edge of the cliff and tossed it down to be out of sight.

The squealing axle of the cart had barely subsided when the jangling of harness hardware became evident on the other side of the roadblock. Precautions taken before ensured that muskets were primed and men were prepared for action at the sound. The outriders came first, ahead of the coach. Four men in the uniform of French Cuirassiers, their bronze breastplates gleaming in the morning sun.

The procession came to a halt upon reaching the entangled branches of the downed trees. Horses rearing, the coach came to a halt. The few men, both outriders and coach passengers, attempted to defend the pouches, but that effort ended when the seamen and Marines came out of the bushes along the road, muskets leveled. A junior officer of cuirassiers extended his sword, as did a major inside the carriage. After seizing the leather pouches of military correspondence, the naval party tossed the captured weapons into the surf, retreated to the boats and were off, leaving the French soldiers to deal with the roadblock.

Next morning, the ship being well at sea, Phillips had Mullins in to translate the captured documents. "Sir, this is all secret French Naval information, codes and the like. I think the admiral would like to see this."

"You're probably right, Mullins. Admiral Howe will likely not be too happy to see us, but we should report this. Make sure you do not divulge any of this to your mates."

It took a week for the Courageous to locate Admiral Howe, but they eventually found one of his frigates and were directed to the new rendezvous. Howe was not at all happy to receive Phillips, but they were finally ordered to proceed to long pistol shot to windward of the flag. The mood was decidedly cool when Phillips went aboard, but warmed soon after.

"Phillips", the admiral asked, "Do you understand the importance of these documents?"

"I have a fair idea, My Lord."

"I want them taken to Portsmouth immediately. Report to the port admiral and do as he orders."

They made a fast passage across the channel and upon reporting, Phillips was soon ordered to post to London with the captured documents. There, handing over the documents after explaining his mission, he waited in an Admiralty office for hours until taken in to a harried man in civilian dress.

The admiralty official, without introducing himself, motioned to a figure standing at the window. "Captain Phillips, please meet Hawkins, from Horse Guards. I'll leave you here to talk."

Hawkins came over and examined the sea officer. Phillips could make no judgment whether the man was either military or civilian. Hawkins spoke for the first time. "Captain, while this package was in your hands, how many people have read the contents?"

"Only one sir, a midshipman named Mullins aboard my ship. He was the only person aboard who could read French."

"You do not read the language yourself?"

"No sir."

"How about later. How many others have read the contents?"

"Sir, I reported to Admiral Howe with them about a week after we took them. I do not know who they were shown to. I was ordered into

Portsmouth, reported to the port admiral there and was then sent to the Admiralty."

"To satisfy your curiosity, Captain, one particular document, among hundreds you brought back, was of major political importance. It is important the French military do not realize this has been captured."

"Sir, I took the pouches from an officer in a carriage guarded by four cuirassiers. I am sure the French officials have been notified by now."

"Captain, the documents were dated several months before the occasion you captured them. We think someone put them furtively in the French military mail for his own reason. We know the person to whom the paper was addressed no longer works in the office the paper was being sent to. For whatever reason, we now have them. Hopefully, the individual mailing the documents will decide to keep his own council. Perhaps he or she will never find out."

"Now, are we clear? You are never to divulge the existence of these papers."

"Sir, I of course will never volunteer the information. However, I am a commissioned naval officer and would be forced to answer any questions by competent authority, unless, of course, I was covered by proper orders."

"Very well Captain. Horse Guards thanks you for the intelligence gift you provided. Goodbye."

Mister Jordan was the next person Phillips saw in the Admiralty building. He said, "My word, Phillips. You do keep popping up." As Phillips started to explain, Jordan held up his hand. "Not another word, sir." he cautioned. "We both know more than we should about a certain subject and it would be better if no one else heard about it from us. Have you heard from Sarah Forsythe yet?"

"No sir, Courageous just returned from the French side of the Channel coast. I posted up here from Portsmouth and reported here this morning. No time to make my manners with anyone."

"Well, she is now living with her uncle near there. Shall I post her informing her of your presence? I am sure she would like to see you again after the last abbreviated meeting."

A tentative meeting arranged with Miss Forsythe in Portsmouth, Phillips had other matters on his mind.

He was sure Courageous was in good hands back in Portsmouth, so decided to pay a quick visit to Mary Harkins. He still felt guilty about his abrupt departure and thought a few minutes spent at the inn would be advised. He engaged a one horse chaise to transport him there. At first glance, all seemed the same after he climbed down at the King's Arms. Then he noticed the sign had a new coat of paint. At the bottom of the sign was penned, "Amos Harkins, Prop."

This was a puzzler. Old Amos was in America, while Mary was now full owner of the inn, having spent money given her by Phillips to purchase the half interest formerly owned by Amos, her dead husband's brother. Why would his name be on the sign?

The driver of the chaise asked, "Would you like me to wait for you, Yer Honor?"

Tossing the man an extra sixpence, Phillips said, "Would you please wait a few minutes? I'll need a few minutes before I decide."

He started for the inn's door, when it opened with a bang and Mary came running out. "John, I didn't expect you. You should have warned me."

He explained to her about the ship being moored in Portsmouth and his being in London on the King's business, but he did now have a few minutes to spare.

"Oh John, you'll never guess at my news. I am married. Old Amos Harkins asked me and I couldn't say no."

Dumbfounded, Phillips stood there a minute. "Mary, a few months ago, Harkins was hiding in America and a solicitor wanted you to buy your brother-law's debt from them. I gave you five hundred guineas to pay them. What happened?"

"Well", she admitted. "I posted him by fast packet that the debt had been paid, so he no longer had to hide. Then he returned and we decided to marry."

"But why him? You owned the inn free and clear. By marrying him, you put him back in the driver's seat as the owner. He can do what he wants to with the property, now."

"Oh, don't scold, John. I needed a man to care for and I knew you would never marry me."

Phillips shook his head in wonder at both Mary and himself. He had thrown away five hundred guineas to assist Mary gain her independence and she had in turn thrown that independence away. He was glad he had the ship. The sea, while sometimes a harsh mistress, was much easier for him to understand than women!

The ordnance people were aboard when he arrived, taking measurements for the long delayed carronade installation. The ship was due to receive four of the big thirty six pounders. Two guns would replace the forward long eighteen pounder guns, while the others went into the enlarged ports occupied now by the after eighteen pounders. In addition, a pair of twelve pounder carronades was to be installed on the quarterdeck.

It being made clear to him that the ordnance crew had little time to spend discussing the armament with him, he went below to go over all the paperwork that had accumulated since his departure. Just below the top, was a letter from Sarah, saying she was staying near Portsmouth with her uncle and hoped to see him. He had just digested that, when the master's mate of the watch reported that a young lady standing by a carriage was waving a handkerchief at the ship. She appeared to be the same lady that came aboard earlier in the year.

Sarah Forsythe came aboard in the company of a middle aged matron who she identified as her dead father's cousin. This lady remained on deck, entertained by the sailing master and several other warrants. After a brief period of socializing, Phillips asked Sarah below to give him advice on possible means of decorating the cabin.

It developed, hours later that, they had spent little time discussing that subject and rather much more exploring each other's personalities.

It was only the Marine's stamp outside his door, with the warning, "First Officer, sir." that brought them to the present. It seemed Miss Arnold, Forthythe's companion wished to return to the carriage.

There was a flurry of activity as the ladies left. Burns hurried up with a packet destined for Admiral Howe, as well as a report that mail bags for the fleet had been left by a boat from the flag while Phillips had been incommunicado. The ship was ordered to leave as soon as wind and tide permitted. An affirmative signal was the only acknowledgement required. It was time to leave.